About Sleepwalkers ...

We do not know what dimensions of meaning and what intriguing situations Mirza Asadullah Khan Ghalib was thinking of when he wrote the line, "Those who have awakened in a dream are still dreaming." About a century later, a novelist of his language, Joginder Paul, lives through a similar poetic experience in his seventy-page novella, *Khwabrau (Sleepwalkers)*. And, if Ghalib had read the novella, he would have been willing to give away his whole diwan for it ... *Khwabrau*, with its intensity and narrative felicity, is indeed a fantastic piece of art.   – *Aajkal*

The irony of an anachronistic perspective pervades the entire novella. In *Khwabrau*, not only has Time been confounded, but the Unity of Places too has been undone. The setting begins by being close to reality but steadily moves closer to dreams ... Joginder Paul has set the dream so perfectly in reality that one cannot be distinguished from the other ...   – *Qaumi Awaaz*

Although the novella has been etched against a Pakistani backdrop and relates a katha of elusive dreams, the image of elemental human violence and the suffering in the katha makes it universal and eternal.   – *Navbharat Times*

Khwabrau depicts the predicament of post-Partition refugees in a way that has never been done before.   – *Dainik Tribune*

OTHER TITLES FROM KATHA

For Literary Connoisseurs
Katha Prize Stories, vols 1-7 edited by Geeta Dharmarajan
A Southern Harvest edited by Githa Hariharan
Visions-Revisions, vols 1 & 2 edited by Keerti Ramachandra
The Wordsmiths edited by Meenakshi Sharma
Masti edited by Ramachandra Sharma
Basheer edited by Vanajam Ravindran
Mauni edited by Lakshmi Holmström
Separate Journeys edited by Geeta Dharmarajan
Mapping Memories edited by Sukrita Paul Kumar

For Academic Use
Books in the *Approaches to Literature in Translation* Series

For Young Adults
A Unique Odyssey: The Story of the United Nations by Geeta Dharmarajan
YuvaKatha, vols 1-8, edited by Geeta Dharmarajan; Keerti Ramachandra

For Children
Hulgul ka Pitara (a teaching/learning kit for Hindi)
Tamasha! (a fun & development quarterly in English & Hindi)
Dhammak Dhum! (a quarterly for pre-schoolers)
Swapnasundari and the Magical Birds of Mithila (in English & Hindi)
The Secrets of Kalindi: A Jigsaw Puzzle Mystery by Geeta Dharmarajan
The Princess with the Longest Hair by Komilla Raote

Easy Readers for Adult Neo-literates (in Hindi)
Abhishaap by Pudhuvai Rā Rajani
Arjun by Mahasweta Devi
Bhola by Rajendra Singh Bedi
Do Haath by Ismat Chughtai
Faisla by Maitreyi Pushpa
Panch Parmeshwar by Premchand
Paro ki Kahani by Sughra Mehdi
Puraskar by Jaishankar Prasad
Samudra Tat Par by O V Vijayan
Sparsh by Jaywant Dalvi
Stree ka Patra by Rabindranath Tagore
Thakavat by Gurbachan Singh Bhullar
Stree Katha (a teaching/learning text, also in Gujarati,
                Kannada, Malayalam, Telugu & Urdu)
Stree Shakti (a teaching/learning text, also in English,
                Kannada & Malayalam)

SLEEPWALKERS

Joginder Paul

Also ...
Essays by Qamar Rais & Wazir Agha
Stories by Ashfaque Ahmad & Sajid Rashid

Edited by
Keerti Ramachandra

KATHA

KATHA PERSPECTIVES

Published by

KATHA

A-3 Sarvodaya Enclave
Sri Aurobindo Marg, New Delhi 110 017
Phone: 6868193, 6521752
Fax: 6514373
E-mail: DELAAB05@giasdl01.vsnl.net.in
Internet address: http://www.katha.org

First published by Katha in March 1998
Second printing, July 2000

KATHA is a registered nonprofit society
devoted to enhancing the pleasures of reading.
KATHA VILASAM is its story research and resource centre.

General Series Editor: Geeta Dharmarajan
In-house Editor: Meenakshi Sharma
In-house Assistant Editor: Dipli Saikia
Design: Arvinder Chawla
Illustrations: Vandana Bist
Production-in-charge: S Ganeshan
Typeset in 11 on 15.5pt Baskerville by Suresh Sharma at Katha
Printed at Param Offsetters, Okhla, New Delhi

ISBN 81-85586-80-2

Contents

Introduction

It is with great pleasure that Katha launches with this volume yet
another series – the Katha Perspectives. If the Katha Classics have,
so far, featured the "grand old men" of short fiction in the regional
languages – Masti, Basheer, Mauni – the Perspectives look to those
pioneering figures of the short story genre, who are still creatively
active. Volumes in this series will attempt to understand the chosen
authors through a sample of their work, both fiction and non-fiction.
Each volume would further include two short stories selected by
the chosen author – a classic work written by a senior writer,
admired by the author, and another story by a person the author
sees as a potential master story teller. To provide a context for the
chosen writer's art, we would also include essays by eminent critics,
discussing the author's literary style and critiquing the work included
in the volume.

The inaugural volume of Katha Perspectives focuses on Joginder
Paul. We begin with a translation of his novella *Khwabrau*
(Sleepwalkers) – the first ever to be published. *Sleepwalkers*, the
story of the mohajir migration to Pakistan after Partition, acquires
a special significance in this fiftieth year of the independence of
India and Pakistan. In this novella, the mohajirs leave Lucknow to
settle in Karachi, but in their hearts they carry not just memories
but homes, streets, chowks, even the Malihabadi mango, and
recreate another Lucknow in Karachi. The immigrants come to
terms with their new location during their waking hours, but in
their sleep, they throng the chowk of Ameenabad. All but Deewane
Maulvi Sahab. His mind, unable to cope with the trauma of shifting,

seeks refuge in a very sane madness, much to the amusement of his family and friends. But Achhi Begum, his wife, does all she can to help him preserve his precarious balance – which is what keeps him alive. Finally, when he returns to rationality once more, he is left with nothing to reconcile to.

Joginder Paul has chosen "Gadaria" (The Goatherd) by Ashfaque Ahmad as a classic of Urdu short fiction. The simple elderly Dauji, a gadaria by birth, proves to be a true "sishya." With perseverance, as well as dedication to his teacher and his Master, Dauji also becomes the ideal "guru" for young Golu. The essence of this story is reflected in the statement, "... how saint-like a really secular person is, and how secular a true saint." But in this intolerant world Dauji has no place. Nor do ethics, morality, religious observances, as Mushtaque finds out, much to his despair, in Sajid Rashid's "Jannat Mein Mahal" (A Palace in Paradise). While Dauji transcends the real world and attains a kind of sainthood, the hapless Mushtaque is torn between the morality represented by his family and religion and the degrading values which he is forced to adopt in order to retain a permanent job in the city. The novella and the two stories are linked thematically in a sense. They all deal with displacement – *Sleepwalkers* with the physical, "The Goatherd" with the religious-spiritual and "A Palace in Paradise" with the ethical-moral.

The two essays by renowned scholars Qamar Rais and Wazir Agha place Joginder Paul and his work in the context of the Urdu short story tradition. This series hopes to allow the readers a peep into the author's mind, understand his creative impulses and share his life experiences. And Joginder Paul's "Self-Obituary" does just that.

I have been fortunate to have had the help of many while working on this book. I would like to say a very special thank you to Geeta Dharmarajan for asking me to edit this volume; to Meenakshi Sharma who is always left to do all the hard work; to Dipli, Shalu, Sanju, Reshma, Arvinder, Vandana, Swapna, Suresh and all the others at Katha; to Ashfaque Ahmad, Sajid Rashid, Wazir Agha and Qamar Rais for allowing us to use their stories and essays in fresh translations; to Sunil, Sukrita, Naghma, Ameena and Naseeb for not letting me use my red pencil overzealously, and for being very prompt with their translations; to Uma and Hemanshu for all that they did for the translation of *Khwabrau*; to Rahman Farooqui for his valuable help and advice; and, most of all, to Joginder and Krishna Paul for their affection, encouragement and support throughout.

The Katha Perspectives are meant to let the writers speak for themselves. Over to you, Joginder Paul ...

March 1998   Keerti Ramachandra

Joginder Paul (b. September 5, 1925)

Sleepwalkers

For Muhammad Ali Siddiqui:
You said to me, Look!
Look this way too!
As I lifted my head
I couldn't move my eyes away

And, for Diwan Barinder Nath (Zafar Payami):
I feel your absence so much!

Sleepwalkers

Joginder Paul

translated by Sunil Trivedi and Sukrita Paul Kumar

One

*T*his is Lucknow.

With the partition of the country the mohajirs migrated from Lucknow to Karachi. And, here too, as soon as they regained some balance, they raised the old chowk of Ameenabad. Here too, tilting their caps in the Lukhnavi style, several streets converge upon the square all at once, as if the whole world were flocking here. When not an inch of space remained in Ameenabad, the mohajirs spread themselves around it. And, in this way, all of Lucknow in Karachi was peopled. Not just the old city, but also the new one born from the womb of the old, was soon spreading its spirit of playfulness over the suburbs. They say people come and go, places stay where they are. But, in this case, the mohajirs had transported an entire city within the folds of their hearts. With some came the bricks of their houses, some carried entire homes, intact. Some brought a whole gali, and others transported the bustling main road beyond the gali – whatever they could contain in their hearts! As soon as they recovered their breath after reaching Karachi, the entire city emerged from their hearts, brick by brick. Who knows what remains at the spot where this city had earlier stood! Here it has acquired such splendour that any visitor to Karachi is repeatedly asked, "Have you seen Lucknow in Karachi?"

In the dying hours of the night, when the silent lanes of Ameenabad are lit with the eerie glow of colourful lamps, people lying deep in sleep in the pitch dark of their homes roam about the bustling Chowk, as if it were day. In the beginning, Manwa Chowkidar would constantly bang his lathi on the road, wide-eyed with fear and astonishment, as he stared at the dazzle around him ... The entire Chowk is deserted; who on Allah's earth do I keep bumping into, in this dead silence? ... What was even stranger was that, within a few days, he actually began to see apparitions. In fact, it so happened that it was only rogues and crooks that the chowkidar could not spot. He could clearly see all the people who had walked to the Chowk through their sleep.

"Arre bhaiya, why are you coming at me like that?" Manwa Chowkidar had leapt back the other night, as he bumped into someone. But then, to his amazement, he realized that it was his

---

Sleepwalkers was first published as *Khwabrau* in Urdu in Lahore (1990). It was made available to Indian readers in monthly instalments in the journal *Shair* in 1990 before the publication of the first Indian edition in 1991.

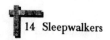

very own Deewane Maulvi Sahab and greeted him courteously, "Assalam-alaikum, Maulvi Saab!"

"Walaikum-assalam, Manwa," Deewane Maulvi Sahab paused for a moment, pulled out a two-rupee note from his pocket and thrust it into Manwa's hand.

"Much obliged, Maulvi Saab! May Allah always grant us your benign shadow!" Even as Manwa was kissing his fingers after saying "Aameen," Deewane Maulvi Sahab vanished into thin air.

"How can that happen, Manwa Chacha?" asked Azizo, the chai-wala, holding out a glass of tea to Manwa Chowkidar.

"Arre bhaiya, if it can't happen, where did this two-rupee note come from?" Manwa took out the new note and showed it to him.

"Who knows? That could have been some ghost or spirit!"

"So what if he was a ghost! He was, after all, our very own Deewane Maulvi Sahab." Manwa Chowkidar paused to sip his tea. "Forget the others, Ajijo, I even saw *you* going towards the bazaar."

"But I was enjoying khwaabe khargosh then, you know!"

"That's exactly what happens! People are out in the streets while they're sleeping in their homes."

"Your mumbo-jumbo is beyond my understanding, Chacha! If people are really walking in the streets while asleep, I'll keep my tea business open even at night."

"I see Deewane Maulvi Saab so clearly in the crowd every night, Ajijo."

"What strange stories you tell, Chacha!"

Khwabe khargosh: Literally, "the sleep of the hare"; this is an allusion to the famous story of the race between a hare and a tortoise. So long and deep was the hare's sleep that the slow-moving tortoise won the race.

Deewane Maulvi Sahab's name is actually Nawab Mirza Kamaluddin, but he is known as Deewane Maulvi Sahab both at home and outside. He is so used to it that if anyone were to call him Nawab Kamaluddin, he would think that the poor fellow had mistaken him for someone else.

While the other mohajirs have created another Lucknow in Karachi, Deewane Maulvi Sahab believes that he continues to live in the old Lucknow, just as before. At first, many of his friends tried to convince him that he had come away from there. But even in the old Lucknow, whenever Deewane Maulvi Sahab had gone out of the city, he would be restless till the time he came back to it. No matter where he went, his journey was always from Lucknow to Lucknow.

His wife Achhi Begum often says, "We had hardly regained our breath after reaching Karachi, when Deewane Maulvi Sahab started pestering us to go back to Lucknow. And, if some good soul asked him what, after all, was left in Lucknow, pat came his reply, Lucknow!"

"Now, what do you do with this?" asks Achhi Begum, continuing her commentary. "Our children are here, our relations are here and all our friends as well. So what's left in Lucknow? Nothing but Lucknow! What in Allah's name would we do there? But who could make Deewane Maulvi Sahab understand this? He wanted to go there precisely because his Lucknow exists only in Lucknow. And where Lucknow is, there must he be."

"Then how did you manage to hold him here?"

"Would he be called deewana if your Deewane Maulvi Sahab were to heed my words!" Achhi Begum herself had given this name to him. No wonder then that when strangers call him by this name, Deewane Maulvi Sahab feels they are his own people. "But all that is over now, bhai. We never returned to Lucknow. Lucknow came to us here."

"Lucknow came here?"

"Of course! What else? It was burnt to ashes, but whatever was left of it followed us here. Such a shrunken little face it had. It was tinier than the smallest section of Ameenabad. Deewane Maulvi Sahab rushed to embrace it, sobbing as he did."

"And then, Begum Sahiba?"

"All of our Lucknow here knows the rest of the story. The ruined Ameenabad began to blossom again. A branch here, then a branch there, and one by one all its branches sprouted. Our Lucknow came alive, exactly as it had been. In fact, prettier than its earlier self."

"Our Deewane Maulvi Sahab never insisted on going back after that?"

"Only the mad know the ways of the mad! Such was his condition that whenever we would ask him to arrange for our visas, so that we could go back and offer prayers at the graves of our ancestors, he would immediately say, Have you left your brains in the grazing fields? Do you believe the graves of our ancestors are located in some foreign land? Arre bhai, we only have to go and offer prayers. Come, let's do it right away. But, seeing me flustered, he would soften and say, My dear Begum, how far do you think our ancestral cemetery is? It is just a couple of streets away. Right behind Nazeerabad is Chhote Mamun ka Maqbara, and to its right, a stone's throw away, is the cemetery. By now I would be imploring him, I don't feel well, Deewane Maulvi Sahab! I don't want to go today. But he would be adamant, Come on. Let our enemies be indisposed. So what if you are feeling slightly unwell? Remember, postponing a pious duty is as bad as committing a sin."

Achhi Begum also talks of how Deewane Maulvi Sahab believes the whole of Lucknow to be out of its mind. He says, "These are strange times. Even in one's own city, one feels stifled, as if one were in an alien land." And, he goes from house to house, counselling everyone, "Arre Mian! Turn to Allah and offer namaaz five times a day with your heart and soul. Can there be a greater misfortune than not feeling at home in your own house?"

"But Maulvi Sahab ... "

"Oh no, Mian. Ifs and Buts won't do! When the whole city is confronted with the same fate, the situation becomes very grave. Who knows, the entire city may have incurred the wrath of Allah for a collective sin!"

"But listen to me, Maulvi Sahab ... "

"What should I listen to, Mian? *You* should listen to me and turn to Allah at once."

The old settlers of Lucknow in Karachi even find some truth in the utterances of the eccentric Deewane Maulvi Sahab. They wonder, "If this is not the wrath of Allah, then why are things as strange as they are? Even after recreating a whole Lucknow, exactly as it was, over this long period of time, why do we still have this gnawing sense of being strangers in our own homes?"

It is not as if the mohajirs have not made any economic progress. In fact, they have outsmarted not only the Sindhis but the other local Pakistanis as well. Through sheer hard work and ingenuity they have grown to dominate business, industry and even the bureaucracy, at both the provincial and national levels. The roads

of Karachi have opened up in all directions. Meerut, Malihabad, Azamgarh and Allahabad can be reached in no time at all.

Four or five years ago, when a cousin of Deewane Maulvi Sahab's came to visit him from the Lucknow in India, his mind split open in wonder. "Quibla Maulvi Sahab, what can I say? I am beginning to feel that the real Lucknow is, in fact, here. And it is not you who have migrated from our place to this, but it's we who have moved from here to there." Expecting to be lauded for his observation, Deewane Maulvi Sahab's cousin looked at him .

"We haven't moved anywhere, Bhai!" Deewane Maulvi Sahab said, suspecting that he was stuck with another one of those lunatics. "Coming and going is the business of tourists like you. Anyway, the same place cannot be situated at two locations. Our Lucknow is the only Lucknow. We don't recognize any other Lucknow. Do you understand?" he said, proffering his silver case to the guest, with a paan with special zafrani tobacco in it. "And, listen. You may find it hard to believe me, Bhai, but you cannot refute the truth. Natives do not just represent their land, they become the native land. If you have any doubts, shall I open my mouth and show you something? Come, come closer, sir – one of Nawab Asifuddaula's thumri mehfil is in progress in my throat! Hee, hee, hee!"

Two

The problem that the mohajirs in Karachi face is that they are compelled to be mohajirs in spite of being permanently resettled here. One or two of them were shocked into insanity and thus freed of these worries. But those who did not go mad have always been puzzled about how they can tune Nawab Asifuddaula's thumri to Sain Bulleshah's kafi on the chimta. A peaceful coexistence of these two discordant musical notes is not possible except through a sympathetic blending. And however effective the sarangi and the chimta may be individually, an abrupt mixing of their divergent notes will undoubtedly produce disharmony and turbulence. In the chaos following Independence and the Partition, this commotion remained subdued. But once the all-pervasive confusion had abated, police rules and surveillance had been enforced, and the mohajirs had started to settle down, this noise was heard loud and clear. In fact, the situation has come to such a pass in recent years that nothing is more audible than the din of riots between the locals and the non-locals. And, if there is a lull, one fears a loud blast will rend one's ears at any moment.

The nawabs of Lucknow, whether actual nawabs or merely in name, cannot help but be aristocratic. So determined and steadfast are they that even if you misguide them on to winding paths and take the easy route yourself, they will still reach the other end much before you and be done with the ritual of their coronation there. You might rush towards them with bombs in your hands, but once you are face to face, their smiles will inevitably disarm you and they will ever so calmly take the bombs out of your hands and put them away. And then, seating themselves beside you, they will patiently invite you to reconciliation and friendship, as if you had gone there not to fight but for that very purpose.

"But it takes two hands to clap, Chando!" says Deewane Maulvi Sahab's son, Nawab Mirza, who lovingly calls his wife Chand Bibi, Chando. He is the general secretary of the Anjuman-e-Ahliyan-e-Lucknow and the proprietor of a big shoe factory where at least one Punjabi, a hundred Sindhis and many Pathans are employed. "The opposition party too should act with patie ace and sagacity, shouldn't it?" he asks as he tries to stretch out on his bed. "Take my workers for instance. Barring a few, the rest are incompetent. They shirk work. And yet, if I threaten to dismiss anyone, they promptly go on a strike without any notice."

"You should never get into discussions with them," Chand Bibi counsels him. "Your work gets done in any case."

"It's not so simple. If I don't do even this much, they will make me pack up! They even claim that the factory is as much theirs as mine. No Chando, they say this not just figuratively, they actually believe it to be a fact. If they were to have their way, not only would they oust Nawab Mirza from his own factory, they would not rest until they had banished him from the city."

"You should close the factory rather than face such bickering every day."

"And where would we go if I closed it? After all, we too have had a hand in building Pakistan. In fact, we are the ones who founded it and gave shape to it."

Finding her husband so distraught, Chand Bibi sits by his side and gently runs her fingers through his hair.

"No matter what we say, Chando, they have a stock reply ... that they are *natives*."

"Look, you dash off to Pakistan every morning ..." Nawab Mirza's factory is located in a Sindhi neighbourhood, away from Lucknow and its satellite towns where the mohajirs live. "Allah forbid, if something goes wrong."

"Don't you worry about me, Chando! No matter where I may be, I am always at home."

"Ha, ha! Ha!" Nawab Mirza's younger brother, Ishaq Mirza, a lawyer, often finds it difficult to suppress his laughter at his brother's words. Ishaq was born in Karachi and educated there. After acquiring a Masters in Law from the University of Karachi, he married a Sindhi girl despite stiff opposition from his family. After that, he had exiled himself from Lucknow and lived with his family in an old Sindhi neighbourhood in Karachi. For almost two years after the nikaah he had not seen his people, but when he learnt of Achhi Amma's grief and the frequent seizures caused by the separation from him, he began visiting Lucknow regularly. Since then, he has been religiously coming here every Thursday evening with his wife and children, returning home only after dinner.

Nawab Mirza is peeved to find Ishaq Mirza laughing at his remark.

"Why do you get so annoyed, Bhaijaan? The real problem with us Lucknow-walas, I mean you Lucknow-walas – since I belong to Karachi – is that you hardly ever venture out of your houses." Ishaq Mirza cannot miss any opportunity to express his opinion.

And Chand Bibi cannot let go of a chance to taunt her brother-in-law. "What are you blabbering about, Ishaq? My poor husband is out of the house practically all day. It is such a relief when he finally gets back home late in the evening. I can't understand why the people of your in-laws' community hound us. They want to flush us all out!"

"The water-taps in the old neighbourhoods are dry, Chand Bhabhi, so how can they flush you out?"

Both Ishaq's brother and sister-in-law feel that he has a loose tongue.

"Why should they want to hound you? They simply want you to identify yourselves with them, be one with them." Ishaq adds.

"No, Bhai! Haven't we given you to them to do that!"

Ishaq is amused by his sister-in-law's bright and playful chatter. "Now look, Bhabhi, and Bhaijaan, you too! Is it fair that we buy out their lands and dwellings with their money, to set up our own Lucknow and Malihabad?"

In Malihabad, just by the side of Lucknow, Hakim Jamaluddin, the maternal uncle of these two brothers, has raised a huge mansion. Ishaq has his mouth open to continue with his narration but his brother cuts him short. "Enough! Stop this nonsense. How have you brought up this absurd point of us using *their* money?"

"Now that the point has been raised, Bhaijaan, you might as well look seriously into the details of the matter yourself. I personally believe that every needy person has a rightful claim on the earnings of a Mussalman. Not only that, it is the duty of a Mussalman to live as a native wherever he is destined to live."

"You are absolutely correct, Quibla Maulvi Sahab!" How could Nawab Mirza resist the temptation to be sarcastic? "Your sermon rains so abundantly here that our house leaks under its force. But there is a drought in the homes of your dear relatives. Why have you denied them your generosity?"

Deewane Maulvi Sahab has a knack for appearing from nowhere just when the brothers are in the middle of their wrangles. Last time too, as they had drawn their daggers, Deewane Maulvi Sahab was seen entering the drawing room. "Ahkhahaa! Khush amadeed, Chhote Nawab Sahab!" Deewane Maulvi Sahab wonders now whether he should join them or first hand over his bag of purchases made in the market to his Begum.

"Assalam-alaikum, Abbajaan!"

"Walaikum-assalam, Beta. All along the way I kept thinking I had forgotten something. Seeing you I remember – today is your day to visit Lucknow."

"That's why I've presented myself here, Abbajaan!"

"Dear Ishaq, whatever you may say, you are very unfortunate! You belong to Lucknow yet you live hundreds of miles away, in Karachi."

As usual, Ishaq just smiles in response.

"Look at this!" Deewane Maulvi Sahab takes out a big ripe mango from his bag and offers it to Ishaq. "Here, have it! A genuine Malihabadi mango."

The taste of mangoes rolls through Ishaq Mirza's mouth. But as soon as he takes it in his hands, his face falls. "But this is made of clay!"

"It's a real Malihabadi!" Deewane Maulvi Sahab laughs. "I bought it from the clayfruit-wala in Chappal Market." Deewane Maulvi Sahab now decides to go in and hand over the bag. "I'll be back."

Just as Deewane Maulvi Sahab turns to leave, Ishaq says, "Here you are, Bhaijaan, try this Malihabadi mango. I challenge you to eat it. Your mouth will be filled with mud."

"Arre Chhote Bhai, who wants to eat it? We are satisfied by just looking at it!"

"No, Bhaijaan, there's no escape from filling one's belly. Don't you find it strange that we eat the mangoes grown here, but our hearts can be satisfied only by the clay mangoes of Malihabad?"

"It's a question of culture, Ishaq Mian. What would you know about the flavour of culture?"

Chand Bibi, who had joined them quietly a little while ago, gets up, bored with their conversation. "Ishaq Bhai, Achhi Amma

gets irritated with the incorrect language your wife speaks. Both of them must be fed up with each other." Then, as if something suddenly flashes through her mind, she screams, "Allah, where are the children? I don't hear any one of them!"

"Let them go where they will, Bhabhi." Ishaq is amused to find his bhabhi pale with fear. "My three children love to come here precisely because of the large open spaces, the full murabba that they get to play in. Once, the younger one asked his mother, Why don't we, too, have such a big ground? His mother lost her temper over this innocent question and started thrashing him, thinking, So what if he is my own son ..." Ishaq paused here and guffawed loudly. "... After all, the child's blasted father is a Lukhnavi Sain! Ha, ha, ha!"

Chand Bibi, also laughing, turns to go into the inner quarters of the haveli.

"The trouble, Ishaq," – Nawab Mirza is still ready with an arrow on the taut bow – "is that you regard culture as just a matter of eating and drinking and having fun."

"But Bhaijaan, you were referring to the flavour of culture." Ishaq Mirza loves to provoke his elder brother on this issue. "But never mind, let me tell you something about my Punjabi neighbour, Fakir Babu. His wife, too, is a Sindhi. She often tells us, Although my husband is a good-for-nothing, once he starts singing *Jhoole Lalan* on the chimta, Bhai Sain, he looks like a fakir padshah. Then our Fakir Babu says in all humility, This Sindhan of mine is a little foolish. How would *I* know how to sing *Jhoole Lalan?* Then, turning to me, he says, Nawab Ishaq,

---

Sain: Used as "sir" by Sindhis. A non-Sindhi would refer to a person from Sindh as a "sain." Also, a Sindhi may say, " I am a Sain" to mean "I am a Sindhi."

you can get me to practise as much agriculture as you like. No matter what you may say, agriculture is the greatest culture. People like you are thrilled by looking at tiny flowers. But just hold a huge cauliflower in your hands and smell it. By Allah, you will start pecking at it passionately, believing it to be the face of your beloved. No, Bhai Nawab, please keep quiet, for Allah's sake. The moment you open your mouth, I fear that you will point out at least ten mistakes in my Urdu ... Whenever I point out to him that it is not Hamara Urdu, but the feminine Hamari Urdu, my Punjabi friend retorts, Arre Bhai, it is so simple. When I speak, it is the masculine, Hamara, and when my Sindhan speaks, it is the feminine, Hamari. But tumhari, your Urdu ... no, it ought to be tumhara, the masculine – what did you say it was? Never mind. Your pure Urdu makes me nervous. What is important is that when we start talking to you Urduwalas we forget what we want to say and we end up speaking like you. But, what is the use of speaking chaste Urdu when what you want to say remains unsaid?"

"But what are you trying to get at, Ishaq Mian?"

"Only this, Bhaijaan, that if the real point of our conversation remains trapped within, then of what use is polished language? If you ask me, I have no qualms about corrupting my tongue."

Three

Nawab Ishaq Mirza is wrong when he says that if you want to eat Malihabadi mangoes in Karachi, all you get is a mouthful of clay. Behind his haveli, in this very Malihabad, Deewane Maulvi Sahab's brother-in-law, Hakim Jamaluddin, after carrying out scores of chemical experiments, has performed the miracle of growing in the soil of Karachi rows and rows of trees of Malihabadi mangoes which are forever laden with blossoms, in and out of season.

Hakim Sahab, by Allah's grace, has been blessed with a large, flourishing family. His six sons and daughters have a bevy of grown-up daughters, so many that he invariably misses out at least one or two each time he tries to count them. And what is more, one or the other is always pregnant.

Hakim Sahab's youngest son, Hashim Ali, works in Saudi Arabia but his family lives with Hakim Sahab. His haveli is so huge that even if all the blessings of the world were showered upon it, it would still have room for more!

The Hakiman, apart from being Hakim Sahab's wife, has no other claims to hikamat. But this in itself is no small thing! Hakim Sahab's entire wealth, even his rare medicinal remedies and prescriptions, remain in her careful custody. No wonder then that, whenever he is in a good mood, Hakim Sahab spontaneously addresses her as his sandookchi, his little treasure chest. It was this sandookchi who carefully carried the plans of the ancestral haveli of Malihabad when they migrated from India. She often recounts with pride, "Hakim Sahab had directed me to leave our various property papers behind with his lawyer. Had I done so, could this wonder of wonders have existed? Even after coming away from there, we continue to live in the same haveli as before."

"Yes, my sandookchi, you are absolutely right. How right you are! The day we occupied this haveli, the spirit of our ancestral haveli too flew here."

"But of course! Positively!" Hakiman responds, holding out a paan to her husband. At the slightest show of anxiety on Hakim Sahab's face, Hakiman knows that he is either looking for his walking stick or his cap, or that he wants to tuck one more paan into his mouth before getting up. "If the spirit has come here, what remains there? A heap of mud?" she adds.

Deewane Maulvi Sahab was ecstatic when he first visited them

here. "Arre Bhai Hakim Sahab, this is wonderful! What magic potion did you use on this rickety old mansion? It looks a new bride once again! I just cannot leave my Lucknow or I would settle down right here."

"Come and live here, Deewane Maulvi Sahab."

"I certainly would, Hakiman, but what if Hakim Mian gives me some poisonous herb by way of medicine?" Deewane Maulvi Sahab teases her just to hear her call him deewana. And when she does, the tassel on his cap bobs up and down before flopping over his earlobes.

"So what, Deewane Maulvi Sahab!" The sandookchi seems to have opened by itself, to give him a glimpse of its interior. "Hakim Sahab also has the antidotes ready!"

In the stylish argot of the Lucknow-walas, Malihabad is a mere arm and a half away, yet "Khuda ki panaah!" exclaims Achhi Begum, "so desolate is the road, Bade Bhaiya, that my heart quivers with fear."

"If your heart were not to quiver, my Achhi Bahan," Hakim Sahab speaks in the manner of detailing one of his prescriptions, "would you come and hug me spontaneously the moment you reach here?"

"The mango trees must have burst into blossom!"

"Forget the blossoms. Hordes upon hordes of little green mangoes have arrived! Go and see for yourself."

"What fun it must be for the black crows then!" Deewane Maulvi Sahab loses no opportunity of attracting the attention of his sister-in law!

"Get away, Deewane Maulvi Sahab! Do you ever think of any thing that's not mad?"

"But he is actually mad, my dear sister in law," Achhi Begum assures Hakiman, resting her forefinger on her right cheek. "Honestly!"

Nawab Hakim Jamaluddin's mansion is known as the Ambion-wali Haveli. Here, high up on the trees, black crows keep cawing, and down below little green mangoes sway on silken threads instead of hanging quietly from the branches. Khuda protect them all, the grand-daughters of Hakim Sahab! Colourful little bundles of mischief, they swing so high – giggling and screaming – that if you see them, your heart skips a beat. "Arre, arre, they're going to fall, they're falling!" The crows bring the sky down with their cawing and Hakiman, shoving aside her paandaan, rushes into the garden. "Arri you ... you shameless good-for-nothings! If you swing so high, you'll all fall outside the walls of the haveli!"

That was exactly what happened two monsoons ago. Shehzadi, the eldest daughter of Hakim Sahab's youngest son, Hashim Ali, came out into the garden in the early hours of dawn. Before she could reach any of the swings a ripe mango, risking its own life, fell on her head as if to warn her. Wait Bibi! Stop. But was she one to heed its warning? She did not stop till she had settled on her swing and then, after catching her breath, with just a couple of swift pushes she swung so high that she sailed over the wall of the haveli and then, hidden under the wings of a dark black crow, she flew away in a flash.

Hakim Sahab spared no efforts to search for his grand-daughter, but he could not find her. But crows are native creatures. And after six, seven months this crow came back on his own, along with his bride.

Pandemonium broke loose in the haveli. Hakim Sahab was just not willing to accept their nikaah. But then, marriages are made in heaven. The moment Hashim Ali heard the news over the telephone, he flew down from Saudi Arabia. Instead of chiding his Shehzadi, he congratulated her on her choice. How does it matter if the groom is a Sindhi or a Bilochi? The important thing is that he is a major in the army, and in four or five years he will be elevated to the rank of colonel and general.

"But Hashim Beta ..."

"No Abba Huzoor. Would you want me to tie my graduate daughter's fate with some petty pen-pushing munshi? No, whatever has happened is just fine."

Hakim Sahab expressed some disapproval initially, but then, finding himself helpless, arranged a grand feast to celebrate the wedding. Even those relatives who had earlier objected to this marriage, joined them in the feast.

It took some talking to convince Deewane Maulvi Sahab that the groom's parents originally belonged to a family of nawabs of Lucknow and that they had been settled on their own estate in Sindh for generations now. "It's all right," Deewane Maulvi Sahab remarked then. "At least they are Lukhnavi nawabs. At worst, they may have lost a bit of their style by now."

Because of his intellectual and literary involvements, Maulvi Sahab had done away with all his fancy nawabi epithets and was content with the simple Maulvi. That is why his heart swelled with joy when he came to know that the groom was exceptionally well-educated. Maulvi Sahab brought several carloads of poets from Lucknow to participate in a mushaira during the feast, hoping that his new relative who was settled so far away from his ancestral place would be happy to get a fresh glimpse of his original culture. But he saw Shehzadi's in-laws dancing the bhangra to the beat of the family dholchi and demonstrating their skill with sword and spear as they approached the marriage pandal and was mortified.

"Do you see it all now?" Hakim Sahab was seething with rage.

"Arre, Hakim Bhai, this Malihabad is so close to Lucknow, just an arm-and-a-half's length away." Now that Deewane Maulvi Sahab had overcome his own disappointment, he was itching for some banter. "But take a look at your own face. You live at a short distance from Lucknow and you've begun to resemble a jackal. So, aren't poor folks who live miles and miles away from Lucknow bound to be jackals?" Finding Hakim Sahab still in a high temper, he began to pat his back, "So what if they are to-ta-lly spoilt now, Hakim Sahab! They are from amongst our own people."

What Deewane Maulvi Sahab unwittingly said to his brother-in-law is what Nawab Ishaq Mirza consciously keeps impressing upon each member of his clan. "Every Pakistani, whoever and whatever he may be, is actually one of us."

In Hakim Sahab's Ambion-wali Haveli, the large brood of Ishaq Mirza's nieces come and sit around their favourite chacha, arranging their zari-trimmed, shimmering dupattas on their heads, leaving their faces uncovered. As they listen to him, they feel they are reading their textbooks which they cannot understand when they try to study them on their own. The same words become so lucid and clear when discussed by their chacha, Chhote Nawab. In fact, many of them have got into the habit of elaborating their chacha's statements in some form or the other while writing answers in their examinations, no matter what the question. And they pass with very good marks too. "Girls, we are all Pakistanis, because we are all inhabitants of the ideology of Pakistan."

"Chhote Nawab Chacha, inhabitants of the ideology ...?"

"Yes, just as we reside in our country, our country too dwells in our minds. If you don't believe me, satisfy yourself by tracing the lines of the idea of Pakistan. An exact and complete map of Pakistan will emerge."

"Wait, Chacha. Let me first get my notebook." Balkees, a student of Political Science Honours, wants to record each and every word uttered by her uncle.

"What are you bringing the notebook for?" butts in Hakiman. "What will you show to your husband's people ... stitching and embroidery, or your notebook? Go, girls, go away all of you!" she scolds and, after they disperse, she turns to Ishaq Mirza. Clapping her hands together in despair, she says "Spare us, Chhote Nawab! Your favourite Shehzadi's doings are already more than we can endure."

Ishaq bursts out laughing, "No, no, my dear Mumanijaan, I am not going to spare you until I have had a paan made by you."

Hakim Sahab had yet to recover from his earlier wound when another calamity struck the haveli. He had always had a lurking fear of thieves and dacoits. Times were bad. Roads were absolutely deserted. What more could thieves ask for? One dark, moonless night they scaled the tall compound walls and broke into the haveli. All six of them were armed with hatchets.

"Somebody should ask these sons of woodchoppers," Hakim Sahab always began his account of the incident with this question, "are men logs of wood to be hacked down? These thieves are quite unskilled, whether it is dying or killing."

"But these are precisely the two jobs they do."

"You are really very strange, sahabzade, what's your name? Aijaz? Aijaz who? Then say so, Aijaz Hussain. One does not learn a job by merely keeping at it, Aijaz Hussain. Every job has a specific technique to it. My late father would say, Only that job is bad which is not done properly. But let me continue ... This sain of ours, I forget his name ..."

"Didn't I tell you, Abbajaan," Hakim Sahab's eldest son, Salamat Ali chips in, more to remind his father of the warning he had given him than to tell him the sain's name, "not to employ and trust any Sindhi sain as a watchman?"

"Yes, Salamat Beta. I actually suffered by not taking your warning seriously. But what else could I have done? He was the only one who seemed suitable for the job. There was this Pathan, too, but one look at him and I panicked. The moment he opened his mouth to speak, it was as if he was charging at me with his lathi. I've already told Munshi Ramdin ... anyway, so much time has lapsed, let another month or two pass ... but you must look for a mohajir; no matter what his caste, he must be a mohajir."

Then his eyes settle on Ishaq Mirza's face, who appears to be smirking, though not without sympathy for Hakim Sahab. "I know very well, Chhote Nawab, why you are smiling. But what I mean by caste is not what is understood by the old-world pandits. For me, caste only signifies ancestry and refinement."

"So, why don't you employ me as your watchman, Mamujaan?"

"That you already are, Vakil Sahab! That is why I am forever worried about losing my property!" Though he doesn't approve of Ishaq Mirza's ways, Hakim Sahab nurses a soft corner for him. "Majha! Yes, that was the chowkidar's name."

"But that's a Punjabi name, Mamujaan."

"All of us know the story, Ishaq Mirza," Nawab Mirza rebukes his younger brother. "Don't interrupt. Let Quibla Sayeed Sahab also hear it in peace."

"No problem, Nawab Mirza." All this while Sayeed Sahab had been busy chewing paan, his changing expressions the only evidence that he has been listening to the story. He has probably finished the paan now. "Explanations do help resolve issues."

"But the detailed explanations presented by our Vakil Sahab have got the police all tangled up like a bunch of fools."

"What do you mean?"

"What else could I mean, Quibla Sayeed Sahab? Call it the magic of our honourable brother's professional argument. On the basis of it the police has come to the conclusion that though the crime of theft has indeed been committed, nobody can be convicted as the thief. When I raised an objection to this, the Inspector told me, Look Sahab, after listening to your Vakil Sahab, we have started to suspect ourselves. If you like, we could put ourselves into the lock-up and hand over the key to you."

"Masha-Allah!" Sayeed Sahab exclaimed. "My late father too was a senior lawyer in Lucknow. He used to say that a lawyer who did not give the police a hard time was no lawyer."

"Listen, there is more to follow," Hakim Ali resumes the story. "That sain Majha first invited the rogues to our orchard for a feast before taking them into the haveli. The mangoes were so deliciously ripe at that time, Sayeed Sahab, that one could savour their taste through the fragrance that came wafting over us. Once, during this very season, the late Josh Malihabadi and some other poets had graced our Ambion-wali Haveli with their presence, on my invitation, for a feast of mangoes. When a basketful of mangoes, fresh from the trees was placed before them, one of his friends told our gardener, Go wash them and bring them quickly. Hazrat-e-Josh Marhum promptly retorted, These are not your verses, Mian, that they will not go down the gullet unless they are repeatedly washed. These are Malihabadi mangoes, straight from Allah's own trees. Washing will soil them!"

"Mamujaan," Ishaq Mirza reminds him, "that story of the thieves ..."

"Oh yes, first listen to that story, Quibla Sayeed Sahab! The thieves may have thought of tasting the mangoes and then getting on with their job. But a very great Hindu sadhu had blessed our ancestors with – what do the Hindus call it – a vardaan, a boon that whosoever savours our delicious mangoes will not remember anything except their exquisite flavour. So once the thieves started feasting on the mangoes, they could not stop. They might have continued till dawn but since the sain Majha was not unaware of the magical effect of our mangoes, he forced those asses to rinse their mouths ..."

"Bhai Hakim Sahab," said Sayeed Sahab, putting another paan into his mouth, "don't use the word ass for people who relish mangoes, otherwise the great poet Mirza Ghalib ..."

"... Otherwise Mirza Ghalib's soul will be tormented!" Hakim Sahab snatches Sayeed Sahab's words away so that he can himself narrate Mirza Ghalib's famous anecdote about mangoes.

But Ishaq Mirza cannot remain silent any longer, "Mamujaan, for Allah's sake, don't start off on Mirza Ghalib's story. We've heard and read that thousands of times!"

"Good things, heard even a thousand times, sound fresh each time." But Hakim Sahab has begun to look a little helpless. "So listen to what followed, Quibla Sayeed Sahab."

"You must be tired, Mamujaan," once again Ishaq interrupts him. "Shall I continue?"

"It is not good to rob the elders of their privilege, beta," Hakim Sahab laughed, but insisted on finishing the story himself. "The story is almost complete now, Sayeed Sahab! Under sain's guidance, the thieves landed right in front of the almirah where all the treasure lay. Forget about other things. A very special sandookchi of ours was also lying there."

"What was so special about this chest, Quibla Hakim Sahab?" Sayeed Sahab was all ears now.

Malihabadi clouds descended on Hakim Sahab's face. "It was to save the sandookchi that I extended this arm. And Jhap! they chopped off my fingers!" He thrust forward his right hand with all four fingers cut off, now supported only by his thumb.

The skies were clear and cloudless, yet Ishaq Mirza suddenly felt as if a mild drizzle had started. He took his uncle's palm in both his hands. "But *our* fingers are yours too, Mamujaan!"

"No, no, Chhote Nawab Beta! Our bodies are our own. We would not exist if they weren't."

Mirza Ghalib's story: There are many anecdotes about Ghalib's love for mangoes. According to one, a friend of his tried to provoke him once by remarking on a donkey which went past a heap of mangoes, ignoring them completely. The friend is believed to have said, "Even a donkey would not eat mangoes." To which Ghalib retorted, "*Only a donkey would not eat mangoes.*"

"But Quibla Hakim Sahab," Sayeed Sahab was now beside himself with curiosity, "what after all was inside that chest?"

"They could have made off with everything else. If only they'd left that one sandookchi behind!"

"But Quibla ..."

"Yes, yes, that's what I was going to tell you. In that sandookchi of your Bhabhi's lay safely our family-tree, going all the way back to twenty generations and written by our ancestors in their own hand generation after generation."

The accident of his uncle losing the family-tree began to amuse Ishaq Mirza and, once again, the sun broke through the patch of cloud. "It's only the family tree the sain fellows have stolen, Mamujaan. Even otherwise, who was going to bother about preserving it after you?"

Four

After weeks of mulling over things, Ishaq Mirza has decided to sit down and write to his maternal cousin today.

Some people are so dear to us that we do not wish to communicate with them in a hurry. Mundane matters, of course, can be talked about casually. We may be constantly conversing with them in our minds, yet we keep waiting for leisure to talk with those to whom we wish to bare our hearts. This is why, often, months pass before Ishaq Mirza writes a letter to Hashim Ali.

"What is it that comes in your way?" Hashim invariably asks him when they meet. "Just pick up a pen and paper and write."

"I would do that if I were to write in your Arabic," Ishaq Mirza retorts, laughing. "But in our language every sentence has scores of meanings. I challenge you ... Can anyone write a single clear sentence in Urdu?"

"You're right. That's why, perhaps, I am unable to write to my dear begum. And she gets so upset."

"We don't face this problem ever, Hashim! My wife writes Urdu in Sindhi and I, Sindhi in Urdu. That is why in our letters we struggle and manage to write only what is essential." Actually, Ishaq Mirza too fears that by not talking about the trivial they may actually end up losing real contact with each other. But, with a vigorous shake of his head, he presses on with his argument, "That is how, due to our incorrect and limited writing, we can understand each other well!"

Hashim Ali has a great fondness for Ishaq Mirza's strange ideas. Now he says, "Yaar, in Saudi Arabia, listening to Arabic all the time and feeling its heat raises my blood pressure. Do you know what I do then? Instead of taking pills and stuff I play a cassette of your gibberish."

Here, Hashim Bhai, I've switched on my cassette ... Ishaq Mirza had written just this one sentence when all those thoughts flooded and jammed his mind. Now he grips the pen and prepares to continue writing the letter.

> Our Deewane Abba Huzoor tells us that in the days
> of his youth, an Arabian horse trader used to be his
> father's close friend. The trader would often come to
> see him and when he did, such would be the condition
> of Mama, our old maid, that she would set aside all

her chores and sit down, reverentially listening to the Arabic flowing from his lips. If he spoke to her to inquire about his morning meal, she would hysterically tell one and all, "I can swear by the Allah-Pak that this noble soul has descended from the heavens. Most of the time he doesn't speak at all. But once he opens his mouth, phar ... phar ... phar ... sacred Arabic flows out."

And look at you, Hashim Mian! Your blood pressure rises higher and higher when you listen to your Arab masters. For all you know, they probably want to express their appreciation of the good work done by you, while you with your mercury high, think that they are trying to find fault. Arre Bhai, why just that illiterate maid, even the most learned choose to hear in the utterances of others only that which they wish to hear. We have this Christian judge in our High Court. Sensing some dramatic turn in the arguments of the lawyers, he suddenly exclaims, "Oh no!" But what our lawyers choose to hear is "Oh yes!" and they gleefully turn even more attentive to their own voices. And this is precisely your problem too. You don't consider it necessary to understand anyone except yourself and certainly not the Arabs – I mean, till they withhold your wages. Me? Arre Bhai, if you were really to understand me, then instead of loving me, you'd want to get rid of me. You don't know I consider you to be a fool of the first order.

Ishaq Mirza smiles and thinks, Hashim is a fool indeed! He keeps claiming that he knows all those rascals inside out, but actually, he doesn't understand even his own children. That is why Shehzadi used to say, "No, Chacha, Abba is a stranger to me. He comes here for two-three days ... When he reaches out to hug me ... I don't know how to say this ... I blush and wriggle out of his arms, although I want to continue holding him. He is my father, no doubt, but he is never at home. Even when he is around, he never spends time with me to try to know me. If *I* am not worthy of it then at least he should help me understand *him*. He mechanically says, Be happy, Shehzadi. What shall I get you from Saudi Arabia next time? ... No, Chacha! My abba seems a stranger. You are my abba ..."

Ishaq Mirza bends over the letter again, engrossed.

> You fool! At least try to be a father to your own children. It is not enough that you won't object if, when they grow up, they decide to marry someone of their own choice. Why don't you keep your wife and children with you? If you can't take them there, and then if you don't come to visit them at all, at least make sure, you are not mentally away from them. I fail to understand what you do there all alone in those seven rooms. When you lie down, do you toss and turn in all seven rooms at the same time? You are living not just one solitude, Mian, but all seven of them. You may think you have made a very sensible arrangement, leaving the children in Mamujaan's care but the children here believe that it's their Dadajaan who needs caring!

If the Ambion-wali Haveli had actually been in Malihabad, Mamujaan's late ancestors too would have herded sheep with great felicity in those age-old and familiar places. What's more, this flock would have included not only the children of the haveli but all your innocent big brothers and their even more innocent wives and ... and Mamujaan himself. But Hashim Ali, this Malihabad of our Karachi, if at all visible, can be seen only from the swing of Mamujaan's imagination. Such a pity, one cannot always remain perched on that swing. What is worse, Mamujaan's family-tree too has been stolen. It is the height of cruelty that the thieves should have wiped off our dear Abba Huzoor's memory as well. So, while Hakim Sahab and Deewane Maulvi Sahab were left screaming, the sheep kept wandering off with merry abandon in whichever direction they turned their heads. What I'd like to know is that even if the thieves had left Mamujaan's family-tree behind, how could our ancestors have herded the sheep homeward through the unfamiliar geography of Karachi?

"Ha, ha, ha!" Ishaq Mirza stops writing the letter to laugh wildly. Just a few days ago he had come across a story in the papers about a girl from some European country having slapped a lawsuit on the Crown. Her contention? Why should she have to write her father's name on an application form for a job? Why should she be expected to know her father's name. Yes, why at all? What does her father have to do with the job, the job which the good woman needs to earn her living? Ha, ha!

Ishaq Mirza feels an urge to give some shape to the future branches of his family tree ... My elder son will go to America to pursue his studies. He is not such a fool as to keep himself buried in books forever. Perhaps he'll fall in love with some junior librarian in his university and then perhaps they'll get married, whether we are able to participate in the wedding or not. No matter how carefully they plan their family after that, they are bound to have at least one child. The child will grow up and then he too will marry and have a child who will also grow up and who knows what name he may have ... "Yes, young man, who was your grandfather? Where was he? What was he?" ... "Sorry, very sorry! I haven't ever given it a thought. As a matter of fact I am only aware of my father's surname since it happens to be my surname too." So there you are, sahab, that is how the whole story of ancestry and genealogy ends. In reality a relationship exists, if it does, in a given moment only, Hashim Bhai, and we sustain such a relationship, in whatever ways we can ... Frightened by his own thoughts, Ishaq Mirza holds the letter in his hands.

> I feel happy talking to you, Hashim, because with you I don't have to bother about organizing my ideas. I blurt out whatever comes to my mind. I am indeed lucky to have a friend like you. When you listen to my prattle so attentively I begin to believe that I am talking a lot of sense. What I probably wanted to say was that changes in beliefs and actions due to changes in time and place are primary and fundamental. We cannot escape them.

> But what do you do about this ... Even after four or five decades of our migration from Lucknow and

Malihabad, we continue to live there. No my dear, I am not talking in metaphorical numbers. Now, listen to an interesting episode. Recently, one of Abbajaan's old acquaintances from Lucknow happened to visit us. Arre Bhai, no, not from this Lucknow here. Now see what a web I have woven! I mean the Lucknow of Hindustan. On the very first day of his stay the gentleman said, "Subahan Allah! Lucknow is actually here! And, having travelled all the way from Lucknow, I have only just reached Lucknow! Over there, we could never figure out where Lucknow had vanished from Lucknow." I submitted, "But, hazrat, where is *your* house in this Lucknow?" For a moment he foundered. Then he surfaced with, "Bhai, the reality of Lucknow lies in the elegance of Lucknow. The Punjabis and Sindhis have so disturbed the rhythm of our Lucknow with the strident banging of their torn dholaks and drums that the city is quite out of tune. Come and see it for yourself. Try to recognize it. Is it still Lucknow or has it become Ludhiana? And if it is indeed Ludhiana, then how do we remain Lukhnavis, sahabzade! Call us Ludhianvis in these changed times. Actually, you are the genuine Lukhnavis, you who have settled in the real Lucknow."

So, Hashim Bhai, do you now realize why the Sindhi gentlemen raise their eyebrows and turn up their noses? Yes, indeed, why else? Because of the so-called Lukhnavi style of ours, the people of Lucknow are able to find their lost Lucknow once

they arrive here. But where should the natives look
for clues to find their own city? Mysterious are the
ways of Allah! Their city, standing solidly in its place,
vanishes. Why and where has it disappeared? Then
what is so shocking about their losing the sense of
right and wrong when they are themselves in a state
of shock? But, speaking honestly, we too deserve some
sympathy. This is precisely what one gains from
history – with a little distance, the entire scenario falls
into just the right focus. Come to think of it, when
both my insane Abba Huzoor and the sane Mamujaan
fought, as if possessed, for the creation of Pakistan,
little did they know that they'd have to abandon
everything and flee their homes. Such was the
upheaval that they locked up their houses and came
away running, carrying the keys with them. In their
panic, it did not occur to them to check who was left
behind inside the houses and who had come with
them ... No, Hashim Bhai, don't laugh! Even if there
is no hope of returning home, one does lock the house
properly before leaving it.

Now listen to what happened after all this. On
reaching Karachi they were stunned to see that the
very houses they had left behind, stood before them.
Since they had carried the keys with them anyway,
they promptly went up to their homes and unlocked
them. Another surprise awaited them inside. They
found the houses naked as newborns, plundered and
pillaged. And not a trace of their brothers, sisters,

mothers, children, friends and lovers, whom they had left behind. Hai! Just try to feel the anguish, Hashim, that you would experience if you finally reached home, only to find it absolutely empty. And everything gone, even the corpses of those left behind, vanished. Just the floors, the walls and the ceiling. Tell me how would you have felt? But why am I asking you to understand all this? After all, you've been going through it ever since you were born. Mumanijaan keeps wiping her spectacles in the hope that suddenly one fine day all her people will become visible to her. No, Hashim Bhai, how is it possible for us not to share the grief of our parents? But how long shall we continue to luxuriate in this mourning? For how long shall we remain mohajirs?

If people from the same society divide into natives and non-natives, sectarianism becomes a permanent scourge. For instance, if non-natives were to become natives, then the natives would become non-natives. Just a few days ago a large number of lawyers had gathered for the annual dinner of our Law Club and we were all having a merry time. But in that large joyous gathering there was this old fellow who sat silently, his lips clamped. He would merely nod his head when spoken to. Ignoring everyone else, I went to him and introduced myself. In response, he too told me his name. He was a Hindu judge by the name of Chandani. After Independence, all his relatives had crossed over to Hindustan but he had stayed

here, insisting that Sindhu-desh was his real home.
What I want to say, Bhai, is that in that whole gathering
he was the only one who did not look a native. And
at that time, it seemed as if the old man was serving
out the collective sentences of all the punishments he
had meted out in his court. I started wondering what
he was doing here when one by one, even his gods
had left this place! And once he had decided to stay
on, he should have evinced faith in his new life, read
the Kalma, worshipped Allah to ensure his
redemption and spent the rest of his days in peace.
Perhaps because he was unable to do so, he kept his
lips locked in silence like a criminal. I pitied the poor
man. One word out of his mouth and he would be
nabbed as an alien in his own Sindhu-desh!

No, Hashim Mian, unlike Chandani we did run
away from there to here, but just like him we hesitate
to step out of our minds. No, it won't do to treat our
minds as prisons. Allah has granted us a mind to
enable us to gain access to the mind of the entire
universe. How does it matter if our location changes?
We breathe where we dwell. Else, we should have
the natural faculty of Hindu sadhus to hold our breath
and yet remain alive. If we want to breathe freely,
there is no other way but to immediately become the
natives of the new place – so native that the natives
who hate us should feel that in hating us they are in
fact hating themselves. Tell me, can my wife be happy
after driving her children's father out of his home?

No, bhai, never. In fact, this is the crux of the matter. Bombs keep exploding every other day in different areas, ours and theirs, precisely because even after four or five decades of physical co-existence, we have mentally been dwelling in our separate planets. You may have seen in the newspapers last week that an extremely dangerous bomb was found lying at the rickshaw stand behind Gunge Nawab. Luckily, somebody happened to see it; otherwise, there would have been a pile of corpses there. Today too, a minor quarrel in the fish market got blown up, leading to incidents of stabbing. Three people died. Six are lying in hospital. Of them two may not survive. Oh, no, it is not important whether those killed belonged to this or that side. What is important is that a few innocents were needlessly killed. No, freedom does not stand for confusion. It seeks its fulfilment through governance for a conscious development and growth of the people. So, there is no escaping discipline if we want to be free.

Ishaq Mirza realizes that he has started philosophizing. Whenever he does, Hashim Ali usually stuffs his ears with his fingers ... "Chhote Nawab, put aside your fake white beard and get out of your theoretical hairsplitting. Talk plainly ..."

"You are foolish, Hashim! When will you ever start thinking?"

"Chhote Nawab, you thinkers have spread hostilities throughout the world and that has made life impossible for decent people like us."

Seeing Hashim Ali get angry, Ishaq Mirza smiles playfully.

All right, respectable brother, if you are bored, I'll take off my white beard and end this letter at once. To always keep you bored is one of the missions in my life. If someone is as capable of getting bored as you are, he cannot remain dull for ever. So you should pray that I bring myself to write my next letter to you soon and that in the meantime I do not become the target of a bullet. Yes Bhai, the situation is so bad that all of a sudden someone starts showering bullets from any corner of a street and, in this game of his, whoever from amongst the passers-by falls, falls forever. Ever since this chaos has become routine, I have started eating and drinking heavily as you do, although you know how I hate watching you gorge like that. That's perhaps why my Punjabi neighbour, Babu Fakir Mohammad often invites me home for dinner now. "Shall I tell you something, Ishaq Bau," he says to me, "You Hindustanis ... excuse me! You are all of course, a hundred percent Pakistani, but for us Punjabwalas, a fellow who is not a Punjabi, is a Hindustani. Excuse me, you are all very fine in your thinking, and we like that very much, but the fineness of your physique, provides no joy to – how do you say in chaste Urdu – one eye or perhaps two eyes or whatever ... We don't approve of thin and short people. After all, menfolk are not supposed to perform Kathak! You must eat and drink well, Ishaq Bau! Become strong! No, no, Ishaq Bau, you'll have to finish this glass of lassi ... So, Hashim my dear, I have

been guzzling down glass after glass of lassi and in the last three months have put on some six pounds. My Sindhan of course feels extremely happy and says gleefully, "Masha-Allah! Now you look exactly like my brother!"

Wassalam!

Five

oday, Deewane Maulvi Sahab has woken up very early and is filled with a pleasant feeling of weightlessness. It is as if a bird has flown out of his mouth and is twittering in the room. Lying in bed, he is unable to contain his laughter, when he thinks, How right Achhi Begum is when she says that I am mad. Does anyone ever laugh like this without any reason?

"You are perfectly right, Achhi Begum!"

In such moments, Deewane Maulvi Sahab is overcome by torrents of love for his Achhi Begum. He is overwhelmed with regard and gratitude for her and feels the ardour of a lover for whom his beloved is all that matters. "You are so very right, Achhi Begum. I am completely mad."

"Go on ..." Achhi Begum swats at the fly on her husband's beard, "Mad may your enemies be! It is out of love that I ..."

"Hai, Achhi Begum, have mercy on me!" At the very mention of matters of the heart, Deewane Maulvi Sahab's hands involuntarily rise to slant his topi. "If my enemies too became mad like me, I would commit suicide at having to share your favours."

Even at this ripe old age, when Achhi Begum places her shrivelled hand on his lips with her still youthful spirit to silence him, he kisses it with such fervour that his dentures almost pop out. In the good old days of the earlier Lucknow too, Achhi Begum had never been able to resist calling her husband "deewana" whenever she felt love welling up in her. "Achhi Begum," Deewane Maulvi Sahab often tells her with great pleasure, "if I remain in my senses even in these last few days of my life, it is only because you call me deewana. Otherwise, who, at this great old age, can tell what is what? Whenever you call me deewana, I feel like rattling off the one and three quarter times tables right up to its sixteenth multiple to you."

"Madder than mad!"

To Deewane Maulvi Sahab, Achhi Begum begins to look just as she did when he'd brought her home as a bride.

In the grey hours of the morning, lying by the side of his Achhi Begum, Deewane Maulvi Sahab keeps laughing and in those few moments he relives his entire life with her, and his past flashes through the murky morning hours. The first time Deewane Maulvi Sahab saw Achhi Begum, she was in her bridal finery and the moment he set eyes on her, he knew that she was the one.

"Which one? Who? Who am I?" Achhi Begum is nervous, wondering if she was someone else, and if he did not tell her, she will never know who breathed in her.

"Arre bhai, who else? The same one I went mad looking for!"

"But you had not seen me before."

"I hadn't, that's why I recognized you the moment I saw you." Deewane Maulvi Sahab has never written any poetry but he has lived it all along. Throughout her life Achhi Begum has sought her identity through Deewane Maulvi Sahab's eyes.

Her parents and brothers and sisters have always complained that once Achho turned her face towards her husband's house, they were left longing to get a glimpse of her. It was not as if she did not feel the pangs of separation from them. So intensely, in fact, did she feel them, that even as her heart leapt with joy in her husband's arms, she was prancing about in her father's home. Achho's father suffered from asthma and whenever he had bouts of breathlessness, instead of taking his medicines, he would call for her and she would come running to him. As she massaged his chest, she would untangle all the knots in his breath one by one, and then, released from his agony, he would fall asleep. And in the quiet relief of sleep, his body looked as pure and unblemished as a new born baby's. Whenever Achhi Begum had some spare time and sat down by herself in her husband's home, the dark rainclouds of Saawan-Bhaadon would gather in her eyes. Thinking of her Abbu, rings of verses escaped from her lips:

> *Hum to babula re*
> *Khoote ki gaiyaan*
> *Jidhar haanko hunk jayen re*
> *Sun more babul re ...*

Silent streaks of lightning shimmered in the dark clouds.

> *Hum to re babul*
> *Pedon ki chidiyan*
> *Raat base uda jayen re*
> *Sun more babul re*
> *Sun more babul re ...*

But instead of Achho's father, it would be her husband listening, standing behind her. And when he appeared in front of her, the pregnant clouds would erupt into a drizzle. "Come, I'll take you to your Abbu's right now," Nawab Kamal would bring his Begum back to herself bit by bit.

"What must my Abbu be going through without me?"

"Come, let's go!"

"I can go, all right," Achho would begin to collect herself, "but if I am away from your eyes, how will anyone see me there?"

He whose fortunes have blessed him with a wife as lovely as Achhi Begum, couldn't help but go crazy, even after becoming a Maulvi. The bird which had flown from Deewane Maulvi Sahab's mouth, has perched itself on the ventilator of his room, and sensing Deewane Maulvi Sahab's attention attracted towards itself, is unable to remain quiet, "Chwee, chwee, choon, choon ... Tweet, tweet. Deewane Maulvi Sahab, do you remember why Achhi Begum came back to you even after she was dead?"

Instead of responding to the bird, Deewane Maulvi Sahab has leaned towards Achhi Begum to attend to her.

Hum to ...: Oh father dear,/ We are but cows tied to your stakes/ Going only where you herd us/ Oh father dear, hear me, do... *Hum to re babul* ...: Father dearest,/ We are but birds in your trees/ Taking wing after a nightly stay/ Oh my father, hear me, do .../ Oh father dear, please listen to me ...

Barely three or four months after they moved into their newly-built Nawab Mahal, Achhi Begum was struck by a viral fever. Deewane Maulvi Sahab nursed her night and day. That night when she lay delirious with fever and the doctors had given up hope, he had knelt by her bedside in prayer and remained in that position till the cheerful rays of the morning sun entered the room. Deewane Maulvi Sahab had felt someone prodding him in his back. When he turned around, he was stunned. Achhi Begum stood there, out of breath, her face colourless. She was trembling with happiness. Deewane Maulvi Sahab embraced her and, still holding her, made her lie down and began offering thanks to Allah.

"Why would I have gone along with the malak-ul-maut, Deewane Maulvi Sahab?" Achhi Begum was exhausted with so much excitement and happiness, yet she felt very relaxed speaking to him. "I set out only because he told me, Come, your Deewane Maulvi Sahab is breathing his last there. I was alarmed, and barefoot and bareheaded, I promptly followed him. I didn't know where he'd brought me. Fearing that I might have been tricked, I felt my heart in my mouth, and ... and then, leaving him, I ran frantically, lost, wandering around I don't know where. In my search for you, I was not even aware that I was dead, and when I regained consciousness, my happiness knew no bounds to see myself standing by you, alive!"

Deewane Maulvi Sahab looks at Achhi Begum lying on the adjacent bed. Drawn to her, he embraces her and she opens her eyes in her sleep and smiles as if she were seeing him in a dream. Then, with her eyes shut, she continues to smile. He wants to

---

Malak-ul-maut: Angel of death.

wake her up but holds his hand back. Let her sleep, she is in the middle of a very sweet dream.

Achhi Begum had similar fears about the treatment of Deewane Maulvi Sahab's insanity. If his pleasant dream were to shatter, he would be a broken man, she felt. Let him live happily in his ancestors' house and city – just as he is – at least he is at peace.

"No, Nawab Mirza!" She did not let her elder son have his way when he wanted to get his father's deranged mind treated. "If he is sane it is because of this madness, so why are you bothered?"

"But Ammijaan ..."

"No, Beta, a treatment which will make him homeless is no treatment for him."

Achhi Begum wipes her tears with her dupatta.

"His make-believe now seems true to me too. Since we and our future generations have to live in this Lucknow, what do we have to do with the earlier Lucknow? If our eyes can discover our past by digging into this land, what is the harm?"

"But Ammijaan, the doctor has assured me that he will be perfectly all right after the treatment."

"No, Nawab Beta, he will get much worse once he is cured!"

Meanwhile Chand Bibi had got Achhi Begum's paandaan ready and placed it before her. "Ammijaan you should stop adding tobacco to your paan. The doctor has asked you not to so many times."

"Ai Beti, what do the doctors know? I eat paan only for the tobacco," she said and, turning her face towards Nawab Mirza, added, "Your Abbu was telling me today, This is really the limit, Begum. After so many years, I don't know what got into me, I took a rickshaw and headed for Kanhaiya ki Bhool-Bhulaiyya. In his childhood, he used to eat Rasalu Halwai's jalebis with great relish at the Chowk. He told me, The whole road has changed so much that not even a trace of anything old is visible ... new marketplaces, new names, new people! I was the only old-timer there, wandering around, lost in my own city, my Lucknow, looking in vain for Kanhaiya ki Bhool-Bhulaiyya ..." Achhi Begum took out a paan leaf from her paandaan and started preparing a paan for herself.

"Promise me, Ammijaan, to do at least this much – chew fewer paans."

"I will try, Nawab," Achhi Begum replied. "But first listen to what your Abbu had to say. He was getting very perplexed about where the Bhool-Bhulaiyya had disappeared but was comforted when I said that the Lucknow had changed with time and that the Bhool-Bhulaiyya was probably just where he had been wandering about. Yes, otherwise why would he get lost there?"

As he got up, Nawab Mirza said once again, "Ammijaan, please let me take him to the doctor."

"No, Beta, I have told you it would be very difficult for him to live outside his dreams."

Deewane Maulvi Sahab's gaze fixes on the face of his wife who stirs a little in her sleep and smiles gently at him. The smile that has been resting on her lips suddenly starts to slide and engulf Deewane Maulvi Sahab.

It is difficult to make out who of the two is asleep and who is awake ... But then, he who is awake is at once asleep and awake. Unable to contain his soundless feelings, he begins to hum:

Api kuan api paniharan
Api gagar ri api gagar
Ahmed piya ki gagar bhar layee re
Bhar layee re ...

As he hums, Deewane Maulvi Sahab hears the door of his room squeak open, and sees his three year old grand-daughter Suraiya crying there. He gets up in a flurry, quickly picks her up and puts her on the bed and asks, "Why is our Surri Beti up so early?"

"My eyes opened, Bade Abbu," she says, holding back tears.

"You have a whole life ahead to open your eyes, Surri beti!" Deewane Maulvi Sahab pauses to ponder over the meaning of his sentence and feels very pleased with himself. "It's very early in the day, Beta, go back to sleep," he draws a sheet over her, right up to her chest.

"No, Bade Abbu, I won't sleep," Surri kicks the sheet off. "Bade Abbu, Dadi Amma is very bad."

"No, Surri," Deewane Maulvi Sahab covers her once again with the sheet, "your Dadi Amma is very good."

"No, Bade Abbu! I slept here last night. Why did she put me back in Ammi's room?"

"So what?" he asks, placing her right next to Achhi Begum. "You can again sleep with your Dadi Amma."

"Dadi Amma, Dadi Amma!" The little girl takes Achhi Begum's face in her little hands. "See, I have come, Dadi Amma!"

Achhi Begum looks at her, half asleep, half awake, "What, you are here again?"

Api kuan ...: The self is itself the well, itself the pitcher-girl,/ And itself the pitcher ... Yes dear, the self is the pitcher,/ I have filled the pitcher for my beloved Ahmed,/ Oh, dear, I have brought it filled to the brim ...

"Yes, Dadi Amma, I will sleep only here."

"All right, sleep."

"But Dadi Amma, I'm not sleepy," Surri tickles her grandmother. "You don't sleep either."

"No, Beti," Deewane Maulvi Sahab coaxes Surri, "Sleep a little longer."

"Then why are you awake, Bade Abbu?" Once again she reaches out for Achhi Begum's head.

"I cannot sleep, Beti."

"I too can't, Bade Abbu."

"Achha baba, here, see! I am going to sleep." He lies down, turning his face towards her. "Now close your eyes."

"No, Bade Abbu ..."

"Go to sleep, Beti!" Achhi Begum again opens her eyes and turns to her side. "Close your eyes, I will sing you a lori."

Surri, lying by her side, starts clapping. "Yes, Dadi Amma. Sing me a lori and I will definitely go to sleep."

Closing her eyes, Achhi Begum begins to sing:

> *Allah, Allah, Allah hoo*
> *Allah hoo, Allah hoo*
> *Joo joo joo – joo joo joo, joo joo joo – joo joo joo,*
> *Allah hoo, Allah hoo ...*

And as she sings the lori, she is not aware that her hand is patting Deewane Maulvi Sahab's head, not Surri's.

Six

$\mathcal{N}$awab Mirza is going out for a picnic with his wife and children. When the cook informs them in the drawing room that everything has been put into the car, Deewane Maulvi Sahab tells his son, "Nawab Mian, go carefully, times are bad." He laughs at what he has said. "In our times too, Abba Huzoor used to say the same. Times have always been bad and have never come round to being good."

"No Abbu," Nawab Mirza stands up seeing his wife rising, "In your times, anybody and everybody wanted to become good." He quietly pushes his point further. "Perhaps, that is why the elite few encouraged evil on the sly."

"Bhai, wonderful! What a fine point, Naw-wab, Naw-wab," Deewane Maulvi Sahab guffaws.

"Aḍaab! Adaab!" Nawab Mirza bows, thanking his father.

"Nawab Mian, don't drive too fast," Achhi Begum warns her son.

"Don't worry Ammijaan. The moment it goes beyond fifty, it simply stops and refuses to budge."

"Arre Mian," Deewane Maulvi Sahab cannot resist quipping, "are you talking about your Ammijaan or the car?"

"Enough of your wisecracks, Deewane Maulvi Sahab," says Achhi Begum, tossing her head. "Go on, Beta, the children must be waiting for you in the car."

Seeing Chand Bibi and Nawab leave the room, Deewane Maulvi Sahab also gets up, "Come, let's sit in the garden for a while, Achhi Begum."

"You go ahead. I'll attend to a few things inside before I join you."

Behind the main building of Nawab Mahal, three steps down, there is a very big garden. Deewane Maulvi Sahab walks towards the rear door of the mansion to go into the garden. Just outside the door is a verandah, and some ten yards from the verandah, in the corner of a patch of tall grass, are roses of various colours. Just as he steps out of the room, he discovers the blooming yellow, pink, red and black roses rushing towards him with cries of joy.

He too advances towards them with quick steps. "Yes, bhai, I'm here with you," he glows with cheer amidst the cluster of roses. "Why are you impatient? If you keep bouncing like this on your stems, you'll fall off."

"Deewane Maulvi Sahab, why didn't you turn up yesterday?" a huge red rose becomes redder as it complains. "My petals wanted to fall yesterday. I pleaded with them, Hey you blessed ones, let our Deewane Maulvi Sahab also see us in our bloom."

Deewane Maulvi Sahab wishes to touch it lovingly, but with the mere desire to touch it, two or three petals fall off, and so he kisses it in his heart. "May you live long!"

"Why do you bless us with long lives, Deewane Maulvi Sahab?" another flower speaks up. "You know we are ephemeral creatures."

"No, dear. You are always playing hide and seek. You disappear from this branch, only to reappear on that one."

Deewane Maulvi Sahab chats with them for a while, and then feels that these colourful little darlings are somewhat tired. Those who don't have mouths and are born to spread their fragrance in silence, when they speak, they do so with all their might and then, almost at once collapse with exhaustion. Deewane Maulvi Sahab watches them drift into the lap of sleep as they talk. Nodding his head fondly, he stealthily slips away towards the other end of the lawn where, in a corner, there is a very old pond. Be it the dry season or the wet, this pond is always full of water, and different kinds of birds keep chirping around it. So soft is the lush green grass of the lawn that he finds it barbaric to trample it under his shoes. He pauses to take off his shoes, puts them in the shoulder-bag dangling from his shoulder, which he considers a part of his attire, and moves with cautious steps, straining his eyes and looking constantly at the ground to avoid crushing some stray insect under his feet.

Suddenly, a forgotten but familiar old face, as old as Age itself, flashes across his mind. Innumerable wrinkles have made Mai

Jasso's face a map of the subcontinent. Even today, Deewane Maulvi Sahab vividly recalls how in his school days as he drew the map of the subcontinent, he invariably thought of Mai Jasso's wrinkles. She used to work for them in the garden. Slipping away from everyone's eyes, he would often go to her grass and straw hut and then both of them would put sugar and dry flour into ant-holes ... Yes! Mai's hut was indeed somewhere here ... He stops, looks around and shaking his head in utter incomprehension, moves ahead. It's been half a century since Mai passed away. In fact a decade more than that! She had been with us ever since I was born. How she doted on me! Deewane Maulvi Sahab chuckles like an infant at his mother's breast, as if he has become a baby once more, kicking his little feet in Mai Jasso's lap. She was such a god-fearing woman.

He wonders where all the Hindus have disappeared but then feels very happy with the thought that by-and-by all of them have embraced Islam. He stops to invoke Allah's blessings of the boundless wealth of abiding faith upon the whole world. Just as he opens his eyes after the prayer, he finds a little squirrel, craning its neck and looking at him, as though it too has participated in the invocation.

"Come here, Bibi!"

"No, you come, if you have the nerve!" She scampers away.

Deewane Maulvi Sahab chases her, oblivious of what he is doing. Just a few steps ahead is the hedge around the lawn. He jumps over it and walks a short distance to reach the pond.

Looking at his reflection in the pond, he somehow reaches the Great Beyond. There's not a soul where he stands, and the proof of his existence lies in the feeling that he too does not exist, that is, not at all, right from his genesis. He finds the feeling very soothing, but through this moment of total peace, runs a wave of anxiety. What will befall Achhi Begum after me? She will cry herself to torture. She will be like a living corpse ... He is very restless ... Merciful Allah, take away Achhi Begum while I am still alive. Without me, every moment will be torture for her. Me? No, Allah, don't you worry about me. Even when she is dead, I won't believe that she is. But my Achhi Begum is too sensible. She won't be able to take it that way. If at all it is necessary for one of us to suffer loneliness, Allah, give me that punishment! Spare my Achhi Begum!

For several months now, the anxiety that their days are numbered has been gnawing at Deewane Maulvi Sahab and now he feels somewhat comforted after addressing his Allah.

On the other side of the pond, Deewane Maulvi Sahab sees a flock of migratory white birds which come here in the beginning of winter, at this very time, who knows from where. They are all so alike that whichever bird one might look at, it seems the same as the one sighted earlier. Around the pond are four tall and dense trees which have probably stood like this, on one leg, at this very spot, for centuries. Like four dervishes deeply immersed in worship, they merge into the land and in fact become the land. And these dervishes have not come from anywhere, nor do they have to go anywhere. Refugee birds from different lands, shivering with cold, come to them for shelter every year and feel free to nest in the warmth of their hair and their beards.

Sitting quietly under the magical shade of these dervishes, with his legs stretched out, Deewane Maulvi Sahab feels very good, thinking of a thriving city of nests in his own head too. He stops his hands from reaching out to his head and tunes his ears to the chyoon-chee-chee, twitter-twitter of the inhabitants of the nests.

This wondrous state is so very pleasing to Deewane Maulvi Sahab that he revels in it for a long time, but suddenly something begins to pull him towards itself as though with a remote control.

He instantly gets up and walks back briskly, arriving amidst the roses in front of the verandah where Achhi Begum has placed two easy chairs and is sitting in one of them, waiting for him.

"Where were you wandering around barefoot?" Achhi Begum says as soon as she sees him. "I am forever afraid, for who knows, where and when you may suddenly disappear!"

"Where does the question of getting lost arise, Achhi Begum?" Deewane Maulvi Sahab takes the shoes out of his bag and puts them on. "No matter where I go, I can never go out of my own self."

"Do you carry this bag around for your shoes?" Achhi Begum asks, laughing.

"Achhi Begum," he pushes his chair close to hers and sits down. "Look into my head – you will discover a whole city of nests."

"Allah! The kind of things you say, Deewane Maulvi Sahab!"

"Don't you believe me? Here, look!" He takes off his topi. "Look!"

"Arre yes, that reminds me," says Achhi Begum. "Last night I caught a louse on your topi. Come here," she asks him to get up. "Sit in front of me, let me take a look."

"Yes, Achhi Begum, it does itch." He gets up at once and sits in front of her. In the gentle midwinter sun, he rests his head in Achhi Begum's lap just as his grand-daughter Surri does and begins to laugh for no reason.

Seven

Not finding anybody at the outer gate of Nawab Mahal, Sain Baba looks around and enters the compound. Walking along the edge of the lawn, he comes and stops right in front of the building. He sees a bell in the verandah and presses it boldly as though people inside the house were waiting for him just then. When nobody responds for a long time, he rings the bell again. This time there is a movement in the folds of the curtain behind the glass door.

From behind the curtain, Achhi Begum asks, "Who is it?"

"It is me."

Achhi Begum wants to draw aside the curtain and see.

"It is me ... aa ... Bibi Sain ... Sain Baba."

"Sain Baba who?" Terrified, Achhi Begum draws the curtains again.

"The cook, aa ... Bibi Sain." The veteran sain knows very well how, when the cook runs away, the women of the house wait impatiently for a new one to turn up. "Ishaq Sain has sent me ... aa ..."

Achhi Begum opens the door at once and adjusting the chaadar over her head, comes out into the verandah. "But Ishaq had said that he would bring you along with him," she says, quickly running her eyes over Sain Baba, as she settles down in an easy chair nearby.

"Now how do I know, Bibi Sain, why he hasn't come along?"

"Why do you have such a big, fat lathi in your hand?" Achhi Begum becomes alert and perhaps thinks of getting up from the chair but she continues to sit. "Do you cook ... with your hands or with the stick?"

"Walking around is ... aa ... easier with the lathi, Bibi Sain!"

In the meanwhile Chand Bibi too comes into the verandah. "Who is it, Achhi Amma?"

"Ishaq has sent us a new cook."

Achhi Begum's daughter-in-law instantly brightens up, but on a closer scrutiny of Sain Baba, her spirits droop. "But this is some sain."

"My name is Sain Baba, aa ... h ... Bibi Sain!"

"Then how are you going to be cooking and all that?" Chand Bibi sits on the chair by her mother-in-law's side.

"I do not know a thing except for cooking, aa ... Bibi Sain!"

Sain Baba sits at their feet and puts his stick beside him. "Murgmusallam, kabab, korma, fish, double ka meetha, namkeen, whatever you want, Bibi Sain. I have actually ... aa ... grown up cooking and feeding people ... aa ... I've done it all my life ... aa ..."

"We don't eat the kind of food you people eat!"

"I know, Bibi Sain. If I didn't know this, the big Khan Sains would have eaten me up instead of the food I cooked when I worked for them." Sain Baba says all this to win their confidence. "Very tough people, they were aa ... but so pleased were they with me that when I fell ill, they didn't eat food cooked by anyone else."

"You are good at telling tall stories, Sain Baba!" Achhi Begum prefers to speak to the servants rather than listen to them. "Only if you actually cook will we get to find out." She has made up her mind to employ Sain Baba. So what if he is a sain? If he is a suitable cook for us, we will make a suitable person out of him.

Though Sain Baba has advised himself to merely say, "Haanji," and keep quiet, but as soon as he gets the opportunity, his wisdom and experience comes springing out of his mouth, "A cook who is no good at cooking up tales, Badi Bibi Sain, such a cook makes very bland food ... aa ... In fact, the first lesson I give to a new cook is this, If you want to make tasty dishes, learn to make interesting tales. But you, of course, know all this, Badi Bibi Sain."

"Yes, we know about that. Too much talking will not be allowed here."

"All right ... if you say so ... aa ... I'll do all my talking within myself."

In the meantime Achhi Begum has gauged the approval in Chand Bibi's mind through her eyes.

"Don't let him slip out of our hands, Achhi Amma."

"Yes, he looks all right. But just remember, he is a sain."

"No, Achhi Amma, I can't have my head buried in the chulha all day. You had better fix it up with him."

"Yes bhai, hold on, we will do so. Why are you so impatient?" Achhi Begum turns towards Sain Baba. He gazes at her, unblinking. "Listen carefully, Sain Baba. This is a big household. We employ only our own people."

"If you employ me, Badi Bibi Sain, how will I remain an outsider after eating your salt ... aa ...?"

"This is the one virtue missing in the salt of Khewra," Chand Bibi retorts.

"No, Chhoti Bibi Sain! There isn't another place in the world that Allah has blessed with a more potent salt."

"I am talking of something else," Chand Bibi begins to explain to him. "Of loyalty. That is why we don't employ anyone except mohajirs."

"Ohho! Chhoti Bibi Sain, I am also a mohajir, aa ..."

"You too ... a mohajir?" Both Achhi Begum and her daughter-in-law are thrilled. But, the very next moment, their faces fall. "But from the way you speak, you appear to belong here."

"Oh sain bibis, nobody in Karanchi belongs to Karanchi."

"Why didn't you tell us right in the beginning that you too are a mohajir?"

"But you didn't ask me, did you!" Sain Baba's entire past rushes into his mouth and there is no way he can prevent it from gushing forth. "I must have been twelve or thirteen when I ran away from my village and came to Sakkhar. What else could I do? There was

---

The salt of Khewra: Khewra is known for its salt mines. This salt is supplied to all of Pakistan and considered more nutritious than sea salt.

not a morsel in the house ... aa ..."

"But you tell us, Sain Baba, that you are a mohajir ..."

"Yes Chhoti Bibi Sain, I am very much a mohajir ... aa ... You must listen to my story first. From Sakkhar, the munshi of a Khan took me to his estate and got me yoked in his kitchen ... aa ... There I worked for full ten years ... ae ... Then, one day, they kicked me out for no fault of mine and I reached Hyderabad where for many years, till Independence, I was a cook with a Hindu doctor. The doctor ran away to Bharat and I was kicked around from door to door all over my Sindhu-desh until finally I came to Karanchi ... aa ..."

"Why have you started narrating this Ramkahani, the story of your life?" Achhi Begum asks, a little peeved. "To cut your story short, you are not a mohajir."

"Don't cut it short, Badi Bibi Sain! I am virtually a mohajir. Here, in Karanchi, all these years I have cooked so much biryani in so many houses that if you made the whole of Karanchi stand in a line and started distributing that biryani it would not finish!"

"We have understood Sain Baba, you are not a mohajir."

"No, Chhoti Bibi Sain, you haven't understood yet. Whenever I stay in the same house continuously for a few months, I feel very happy. I start to believe, Now only my dead body will leave this place. But in just a year or two, I am thrown out ... aa ..."

"But why do they turn you out?" Achhi Begum is all ears.

"Don't know ... aa ... My earlier master was also from Nukhlow, just like you ... ae ... A month and a half ago he sacked me because nowadays there are too many riots between Sindhis and the Nukhlow-walas all over the city."

Achhi Begum and Chand Bibi once again exchange, through

their eyes, the fear they share about him.

"Now, you tell me, a man who makes tea and cooks food all day long, will he pay attention to the riots in the town or to the water boiling and storming in the pot? My riots are constantly going on in the kitchen ... aa ... I hear the sound of guns only on the days when I'm thrown out on the roads ... ae ..."

"Sain Baba, this is after all the responsibility of an entire household and not just some office or shop. We are actually looking for a mohajir cook."

"I have no home, no neighbourhood, no bonds with the past or the future! For the past six weeks I have been knocking on one door after another for shelter ... aa ... Because I am a mohajir, isn't it ... ae ...?"

Seeing Sain Baba getting up dejected, Chand Bibi is startled and, this time, instead of advising through her eyes, she speaks aloud to her mother-in-law, "Achhi Amma, wasn't Nawab Mirza telling us that these mohajirs of ours have begun to put on airs! They will not take up domestic jobs like making rotis!"

Achhi Begum gestures to her daughter-in-law to keep quiet, and addresses Sain Baba, "Keep sitting, Sain Baba. After all you have been sent here by our Ishaq Mian and obviously, he would have made inquiries about you before sending you to us."

Sain Baba is so overwhelmed with joy that he finds it difficult to stand up. "Forget about all this inquiry business ... aa ... I am a very good person ... aa ... And Ishaq Sain is so simple and innocent that he cannot tell a crook from a gentleman. He asked me to meet you the very day I was thrown out by the Nukhlavi Sain. Actually I had lost his address. As soon as I found it yesterday, I went running to him ... ae ..."

"All right, you can start from today itself." Achhi Begum announces her decision to him. "Your salary will be decided after my elder son returns from work in the evening."

"May Allah grant you a long life ... ae ... Badi Bibi Sain!"

"Go, fetch your clothes and things."

"I have just these three clothes ... aa ... that I am wearing. Besides them, I have only the name of Allah ... aa ..."

"Arre, you are really a mohajir, Sain Baba."

"That's what I have been telling you ... aa ... Chhoti Bibi Sain," and then with renewed enthusiasm, his manner becomes more relaxed and free. "In truth, we are all mohajirs ... ae ... Who knows where Allah will send us after we've breathed our last ... aa ...?"

Suddenly Achhi Begum raises her eyes towards the gate from where Deewane Maulvi Sahab has entered with such speed that he seems to be walking ahead of himself. Leaving Sain Baba there, Achhi Begum goes to the edge of the verandah and stands with her face towards Deewane Maulvi Sahab. From that distance, he raises his arm and shakes his bag, then, he starts walking faster and is soon gasping for breath. "Pede, Achhi Begum! I have brought Allahabadi pede, look ..." he opens his bag right under her nose.

"What a delightful aroma, Deewane Maulvi Sahab!"

"And why not, Achhi Begum? After all, these are Allahabadi guavas. Such seeds would give up their lives if planted even two miles away from Allahabad!" says Deewane Maulvi Sahab with a lot of pride. "Hold one in your hand and see how smoothly it glides through your fingers. Naddu Allahabadi was sitting with

---

Pede: Traditional sweets, made of milk products. Here, the delicious mangoes of Allahabad are likened to pede by Deewane Maulvi Sahab.

heaps and heaps of them near Agha Mir ki Dyorhi, calling out,
Unveiled they lie here, take them in mounds ... So Achhi Begum,
don't ask me the price, just taste them ..." He is surprised to see
Sain Baba. "Who are you, Mian?"

"Your new cook ... aa ... Bade Maulvi Sain."

Achhi Begum tells him that Sain Baba has been sent by Ishaq
Mirza and that she has already employed him.

Deewane Maulvi Sahab looks at Sain Baba carefully. "You seem
to belong to Sindh-vindh?"

"Ji haan, Bade Maulvi Sain!"

"Can't you people get jobs in your own native place?"

"It is very difficult, aa ... Sain." Sain Baba is not sure what answer
Deewane Maulvi Sahab expects from him.

"That is why a large number of Sindhi and Punjabi mohajirs
have come and settled around us," says Deewane Maulvi Sahab,
moving to the door behind Achhi Begum. Once again he turns
towards Sain Baba. "Work with all your heart, bhaiya. Lucknow
beckons only the fortunate."

Eight

Yes, Hashim, my very dear friend, I have received all the letters you wrote me during the last two months but what do I do? Not one of them contained anything from the heart or at least anything that truly matters. This letter is not in reply to any of yours. I am actually fulfilling my desire to meet you. It is not incorrect to say that writing frequently is not quite the same as meeting freely, but reading what *you* write only increases the distance between us. You heartless creature, stop tormenting me by writing these letters. Take some time off and come yourself instead ...

Ishaq Mirza stops writing and muses, Yes indeed, it would be great fun if Hashim could come. It has been a long time since I turned towards Lahore and Peshawar. As soon as he comes, I will bundle him up in my car and only after crossing Hyderabad will I tell him where we are headed. While he keeps screaming and swearing by Allah that he must get back to Saudi Arabia within four days, I shall take him even beyond Bahawalpur and Multan ... We will take Babu Fakir Mohammad along with us. The more the merrier!

"Come on Bau, shall we go to your village?"

"Oh yaara, do you even need to ask? Come on! Let's go, let's go just now!" This is why Ishaq Mirza holds the Punjabis dear to his heart. So tough in the body, so soft in the heart. Touch their hearts a little and you can pull out whatever you want!

Last year, Ishaq Mirza's wife's younger sister got married to a burly, moustached Punjabi zamindar. "Kulsoom, do something about your Chowdhary's moustache," Ishaq Mirza had told her once, "they hurt the eyes!" She had said, "I too used to feel scared, Dulhe Bhai, wondering how long I would be able to ride this tiger! My eyes too would be sore but he told me, This is a crop ready for harvesting, Bibi. Your heart should leap with joy looking at it!"

"But, Kulsoom ..."

"No, Dulhe Bhai, come to our village some time. You will forever treasure the sight of our harvests!"

Ishaq Mirza decides to visit Kulsoom's village, too, during the trip.

He gets back to the letter again.

> Hashim yaar, it has just occurred to me that this time
> when you visit Malihabad, I'll dupe you into going to
> Punjab and towards the border with me. Now that I

have mentioned it to you, let it be absolutely clear that, come what may, you have to go there. If you say No, I will tie you up and carry you along with me. Bhabhi tells me you start harping about going back as soon as you arrive and she remains quiet because she does not want to commit the sin of holding back a person bound for Yasrab Nagri, but you don't go there with the pious intention of Haj, do you? You, of course, are drawn by the lure of money, and saving anybody from greed is after all a pious act. This time you must come here on long leave. We will travel in my car and not by rail or air. We will take Babu Fakir Mohammad along with us. He is a very friendly sort. Babu is from Sialkot, the city of our great poet Iqbal. We shall wander about the lanes of a city which has produced great people and where our beloved poet saw the shadows of his future ideas. Babu Fakir Mohammad says that as soon as he returns to his city, he involuntarily turns to his forgotten namaaz.

Yes, we will get to Lahore even before we reach Sialkot. You must have heard the saying, He who has not seen Lahore is not yet born ... I know, I know. You have seen Lahore but in your case, even after seeing Lahore you have remained unborn. Hashim Bhai, as a child, holding your Abbujaan's hand, you can't get to see even the only bazaar of your little Malihabad, leave alone Lahore. This is the reason why you are yet to be born even though you are the

father of four daughters. This reminds me, our dear
Shehzadi has written to me from Bannu. Her husband
is now a Lieutenant Colonel. During the British Raj,
our elders used to flaunt their ribbons for the ranks
of Jamadar or Subedar with great pride. Now our
youngsters have got so many opportunities to
demonstrate their talents. One can go as far as one
wants. Yes, entirely on one's own strength! I can see
your sarcastic smile, but just think ... it is no mean
achievement that we have been successful in scaling
racial walls and, even if only in principle, every citizen
of our country can keep running the race, for as long
as his breath allows him. It is no ordinary thing that
the field has opened up for more people.

The fact is that Hashim Ali had left the country because, here,
he could not get a job that matched his training and competence.
Whenever there was a chance of success, someone at the top would
pull strings in favour of some other candidate and Hashim Ali
would be left cursing his fate. At that time, Ishaq Mirza had talked
about the increasing opportunities for the Pakistani citizen to race
ahead. Of what use is such a race? Hashim Ali had replied, seething
in frustration. In this mad scramble, one keeps getting back to the
same point where one started, even after a lifetime's hectic running.

Ishaq Mirza wanted to always face the bitter truth of his cousin's
statement. He wanted to confront reality squarely, like a true
Muslim, rather than run away from it. He continued with the letter.

For the progress of a community, every new
generation has to take over from where the previous

generation left off. If today we have to face many hardships in battling with the ills in society, let us not forget that our suffering will spare our children a similar fate. You had better suffer your own hardships and let them cope with theirs. Now, what is this whirl I have landed myself in, Hashim? If only you could understand what I say, it wouldn't get so complicated. But then, what is the harm? As you say, the good thing about all whirls and circles is that we always come back exactly to the same spot from where we started.

Shehzadi has also mentioned in her letter that her husband might be sent to our embassy in Delhi for about six months, as a temporary assistant to the Military Attache. Her husband wants to take her along but who knows why Shehzadi is reluctant. I will write to her that she must accompany him. Isn't it a fact, Hashim, that the obvious cause of the tragedy common to both countries is the suspicion and mistrust with which we unnecessarily keep charging each other? The coming generations can be relieved of this misfortune only if the youth from both sides meet frequently. And, if at all they must fight, they should quarrel at the personal level and not fight national wars. Let them fight to their hearts' content, in anger or in love, but they must keep meeting each other. This is true not only of the people of two neighbouring countries, but also of married couples. If a couple took a vow not to meet each other for

years, they might not officially be divorced ever, yet
the relationship will eventually dry up and die. And
then, if they ever happen to meet, each one will
enquire about the whereabouts of the other! They
do not realize that if the other is not in one's heart,
one cannot meet him or her anywhere else.

No, Hashim Ali, I am not joking. If you think that
such a thing can never happen, listen to me and see
how everything is possible. A young man from Quetta
got a job some three and a half decades ago, here in
Karachi. His salary was meagre, so the poor fellow
kept sending money home and postponing his visit
in the hope that he would be able to go home the
following year. Thirty-five years went by this way and
finally, when he retired, he was left with no option
but to go home. He went back and knocked at the
door. Finding his young wife at the door, he embraced
her without uttering a word and, moments later, was
extremely embarrassed to discover that she was his
thirty-four year old unmarried daughter and that his
old wife was lying ill! Wait, there is more. Inside, the
old wife was lying on the cot, writhing with an ache
in her kidneys. When she saw him she said, Have
you come from Karachi, bhai? Tell me all about the
doings of my husband. I hear he has kept three wives
and is playing around with so much wealth that if the
Shariat were to allow it, he would have three more ...
No, Hashim, no. Even if it is just a concoction, you
cannot laugh it away, as long as it is not irrelevant.

Those who do not meet at all, how can they ever understand each other? Yes, you are right when you say that people often become perfect strangers to each other even while living together for years. But that is a different matter. What we are actually arguing is, why meeting is essential for love.

Ishaq Mirza smiles and holds back his pen. Should he remind his friend of how, in his youth, Hashim was all set to commit suicide because of his unrequited love for Rehana and yet, soon after his meetings with her came to an end, he was so excited about his marriage to someone else that he kept producing children in quick succession?

Ishaq Mirza feels the Indo-Pak issue slipping away from his pen, and he grips the pen firmly between his fingers.

Isn't this your observation as well, Hashim? Our elders, so badly are they trapped in the nostalgia of Hindustan that, unless they label even the local mangoes as Malihabadi mangoes, they do not consider them worth a paisa. And our youngsters, they believe that Hindus do not eat animal meat, all they eat is leaves and grass or human flesh! See how ridiculous the thinking of the inhabitants of these two countries sharing the same history is! On the one hand are the developed nations of Europe where scores of trains move freely from one country to another as if they were passing through one city after another in the same country, and on the other hand are the citizens of these two unfortunate neighbouring countries who avoid crossing over from here to there even in their imagination, for fear of being nabbed for not possessing visas.

It should be one of the foremost responsibilities of our governments, Hashim, to put aside temporary gains and relax entry regulations for each other. Otherwise, instead of flourishing, the natural abilities of the terrorized people will get cruelly stifled.

Just the other day a young Hindustani Sindhi lawyer was here to see his father's old house and city. He had brought with him a letter of introduction from a common friend so that I might give him all the help possible during his stay here, which I wanted to anyway. He had only visited me once for dinner when some officer from the Intelligence began to hover above me. What is your relationship with him? He kept pestering me with the same query. And when I finally told him that I had read classical Persian love poetry only at a very tender age, he did not understand my allusion and was furious. He said, What have I been asking you and what are you replying to? His men followed me for several days after that. To tell you the truth, fearful of his colleagues, I did not contact that rather nice boy even on the phone, after that one dinner. He must have thought us to be very rude ...

And when ... my allusion: Ishaq Mirza is referring to that strain of classical Persian poetry which tells of the love between two men – the story of Mahmud Ghaznavi and Ayaz, for instance.

Now listen to another one. My clerk has recently returned from Azamgarh in Hindustan. He told me he had gone there after about twenty years to meet his mother, sister and brother. When the CID over there came to know of his arrival, they wanted to know from his mother why her son had come to see her! They wanted to make sure that the innocent eagerness of a son to see his mother after a separation of twenty years was not, in fact, the preparation for a major international conspiracy ...

Have we gone mad? No Hashim, mad people are extremely harmless, like our insane Abbu. I consider Abbu's insanity as nothing less than a blessing. Why should he go there to see his dear old Lucknow? There is but one Lucknow in the whole world and that Lucknow is here in Karachi ... Wait a minute, Hashim, I am overcome ...

Earlier, Ishaq Mirza too, like his elder brother, had suggested that Abbu be put under medical care, but after listening to Achhi Amma, he was convinced that the cure for his father's insanity lay in the malady itself. When an illness becomes serious, then, by Allah's grace, from the illness itself emerges its cure.

Ishaq Mirza becomes impatient with the desire to forcibly inject a dose of madness into all the mohajirs who crave a visit to their lost homelands. Just a small prick – after which, liberated from the rigours of official doubts and queries, they would blissfully live in their original abodes. Insane people are so pure, so innocent and carefree that even the harshest of governments would feel ashamed once it looks into their eyes.

Ishaq Mirza is overcome by a deep sadness. He wants to sit for some time, silently, doing nothing, and, putting his pen on the table, he decides that he will complete the letter in a day or two.

Nine

Ishaq Mirza and his Punjabi neighbour, Babu Fakir Mohammad, are returning home in Ishaq's car after having dinner at Nawab Mahal. This last week Ishaq Mirza's son has been a little under the weather, which is why he had taken Babu Fakir Mohammad there instead of his wife and children. Finding the road clear and open, Ishaq presses the accelerator and says to his friend, "The way Bhaijaan talks! He sounds like he is giving a discourse."

"Yes, Ishaq Bau, I was at my wit's end listening to him."

Ishaq Mirza laughs at this. "But I was enjoying myself thoroughly. Our dainty little Nawab Mirza was lampooning the

Punjabis in his own inimitable style and you big swaggering Punjabi, you were listening to him, your head hanging down. I get such a thrill to see the physically stronger person feeling so helpless!"

"Look ahead, Bau!"

Alert, Ishaq Mirza grips the steering wheel firmly and sighting a blind turn on the road ahead, reduces the speed. "Why were you so quiet?"

"I thought you were arguing on my behalf."

"Then where is my lawyer's fee?"

"Your wife will be visiting her parents next month, but you will be getting your roti as usual, that is no small thing!"

"You're using the rude *tumhari roti*, Fakir Babu! Don't let your tongue get impious."

"But Bau Ishaq, the holy name of Maula is at the tip of my tongue every moment, breath after breath!" Fakir Mohammad retorts, and starts laughing.

"With me you are so spirited, so why were you scared there?"

"It's different with you. Speaking in Urdu with you is like speaking in my own tongue. But Nawab Sahab talks all sorts of nonsense in his chaste Urdu. Listening to him makes me very nervous!"

"Good you've told me. Now, whenever I see you getting a bit too cheeky, I will promptly drive you down to Bhaijaan's and present you in his service."

"Try to understand my point, Bau Ishaq. As they say, One who knows the language well always sounds correct even if he is absurdly wrong, and one who does not know it sounds absurd even though he might be saying that which is right. Drive carefully, Ishaq Bau!" he warns once again, as he sees Ishaq Mirza going off the road.

"You mean that is why you Punjabis would rather use your hands and feet to speak than the mouth?"

"Precisely! What else? Otherwise simple people like us would appear either false or dumb!"

"But my very dear friend, it is animals who speak through their limbs!"

"But that is because the poor creatures cannot speak, Bau Ishaq!" Babu Fakir Mohammad replies rather sharply. "Say what you will, the purpose is to communicate, no matter how!"

Ten

At the Bagh Goongey Nawab crossing, Manwa Chowkidar tries to slip by without being seen by Azizo, the chai-wala. But Azizo spots him and shouts after him, "Where are you trying to steal away, Manwa Chacha? Won't you have any tea today?"

"How can I?"

Manwa comes and sits near Azizo.

"Allah forbid, is anything wrong with your mouth?"

"What will I do with a healthy mouth if I don't have any money?"

"Chacha, you belong to Sitapur, my hometown. When have I ever asked you for money?"

Azizo starts making tea for him.

"But shall I ask you something, Chacha? Where does all your money go? You are forever complaining."

"Where will it go? Isn't your great Chachi sitting in the house?" As he watches Azizo put sugar in the empty cup, Manwa Chowkidar seems to be already drinking it. "That is why I tell everyone, Do whatever you will, but never get married!"

"No, Chacha. If it were not for my wife," Azizo holds out the cup of tea to Manwa, "I would be finished. But let's talk about something else."

"Right!" Taking the cup in both hands, Manwa too starts thinking fondly of his wife. "Wife ... yes ... no matter what kind she is, she is one's own after all ... So what is the news? Any more bomb blasts?"

"No, no. Wasn't yesterday's bad enough? The walls of all of Nukhlow are still in tremors." Azizo has made a cup of tea for himself as well. "It exploded on the roof of the Zamindoz Chai-khana. Three people and a eunuch were blown to bits."

"Eunuchs are people too. Why do you think of them as being different?"

"Yes, Manwa Chacha, the poor chap's fate led him there. Just a little before going there he had had a cup of tea with me here. How was he to know that he was drinking his last cup of tea! Neither did I know, otherwise I would have given him a special."

Stretching his legs comfortably on the pavement, Azizo gulps down a big mouthful of tea. "How do I tell you Chacha? The chap was so colourful. My wife would always taunt me, Did that aunt of yours turn up today also? Wah! What a man! He has gone and got himself killed and, in the bargain, the rascal has killed us too!"

"Why are these sain fellows hounding us like this?"

"Because we are so desirable! Ha, ha, ha!"

Who knows whether Manwa is angry at seeing Azizo laugh, or upset to see his tea finish in just two gulps. "Not everything is to be laughed off with your hee-hee, Ajijo."

Azizo realizes that Manwa is not satisfied. "Here, I will make one more cup for you. You know very well, Chacha, my wife too is a daughter of these local sains. I asked her, Why are those sains of yours creating such a ruckus? She said, Where would paupers like us get bombs that cost thousands and lakhs, you stupid sain? All this is really the work of the rich sains and mohajirs sitting high up there ... "

"Now look at this nonsense! Why should our mohajirs go about blowing up their own people?"

"They say women have their brains in their heels, Chacha. Ignore her," Azizo assumes the posture of a political leader trying to get to the root of the matter.

"This is what we should be thinking about – Who is our own and who an alien. I do not consider even my wife to be my own. Just four days without any money for food and she'd turn me out of the house!" He comes closer to Manwa Chowkidar. "Leave her alone, Chacha! Give me one lakh rupees and you can even get my head chopped off. Agreed?"

Meanwhile, Azizo sees another customer of his whiz past them. He calls out, "Arre, Kallan Mian! Won't you have tea? I shall make it so sweet that a stream of honey will start flowing."

"No, Azizo, I am in a hurry today."

After Kallan has moved ahead, Azizo says, "Manwa Chacha, our khadi boli is very sweet, but it is great fun to speak the Urdu of Nukhlow city with Kallan Mian."

After a while he complains, "No bloody customer is stopping

here today. My father calls me Ajijo because I ... I am not just one, I am equal to ten. But what is the use? Though ten in one, I do not earn enough even for one! I wish someone would blow me off with a bomb," he takes the last gulp from his cup. "Or I knock ten of them off, either ours or theirs." He washes his empty cup. "I am telling you all this because you happen to be a night watchman. What do you know of the wild storms that keep raging throughout the day in these small tea cups?" He picks up the first cup emptied by Manwa Chowkidar for washing. "Anyway, that is all the news of the day. Now you give me the news of the night. You say that the whole of Nukhlow comes down into the bazaar in dreams."

"Yes, Ajijo, I actually sat down to tell you about the incidents of last night, and I forgot all about it in our chatter." Before starting his tale, Manwa pauses for the last slurp of his second cup of tea.

"Start then, Chacha."

"Last night was the limit, bhaiya! Hordes of people kept gathering on the ground in the middle of Haphat Rahe and soon there was not an inch of space left. I made inquiries from a venerable white-bearded man and was told that the bombs which exploded the other day near the tea-stall have caused serious trouble in and around Nukhlow. Now all the people, led by Deewane Maulvi Sahab, were going in a procession to Laat Sahab's bungalow ..."

"Ha, ha, ha, ha ..." Azizo breaks into wild guffaws. "Very interesting news this, Chacha Manwa. What should happen during the waking hours of the day has been done by these fellows in their sleep. Ha, ha ...!"

Ajijo: Plural of Ajij, a distortion of the name Aziz. To tell a child that she or he is precious, parents often say things like, "For me, you are not one but as valuable as ten put together."

"You just ha-ha but each and everyone from Nukhlow, infants and all, reached here through their sleep."

"Hee ... hee ... hee ..."

"Ajijo, if you keep hee-hee-ing like that, I'll end my story just now."

"No, Chacha, carry on."

"My mind started to work like a thief's ..."

"Chacha, if a watchman starts thinking like a thief, then Allah protect us."

"Don't interrupt. I did have a wicked thought, but I told myself, No, this will not do, Manwa. You are the only one who is awake. If you want to join their procession, you first go and sleep like them. So I went into the dark lane of Lalloo Nanbai, and there, on a small platform, I stretched out, wrapped from head to toe in a chaadar. My limbs were already aching with fatigue. The moment I wrapped the sheet around myself, I fell asleep. And then, then I joined the procession directly in my sleep. The procession was already on the move. Jostling through the crowd, I somehow managed to reach Deewane Maulvi Sahab. How shall I describe his glory! The small tassel of his Turkish cap was fluttering like the flag of Jehad in the red dust storm. In the beginning, Maulvi Sahab shouted Nara-e-takbeer in his booming voice. Then suddenly – who knows what occurred to him – with all his might, he screamed into the loudspeaker, We shall have ...! And do you know, Ajijo, what the entire procession cried out in one voice? Pakistan! Pakistan! What happened after that is absolutely incredible. Though these ears have heard and these eyes have seen it all, I still cannot believe it. Deewane Maulvi Sahab was, in any case, even more insane. He does not know that it has been nearly half a century since Pakistan was created. But just think, Ajijo, what was wrong with the whole crowd? Had it also gone mad with the bombs and explosives? Arre bhaiya, forget the crowds. What was wrong with me? It seemed as if the days before Independence were here again, and a similar procession of the fearless was out on the streets of Nukhlow. And, they were vigorously shouting slogans:

> *Le ke rahenge Pakistan!*
> *Pakistan! Pakistan!*
> *Pakistan ka matlab kya?*
> *La Ilaha Illallah!*

Le ke ...: We shall have Pakistan!/ Pakistan! Pakistan!/ And what does it mean, Pakistan?/ There is no other god save Allah!

Eleven

About one and a half furlongs away from Nawab Mahal, Deewane Maulvi Sahab sits chatting with his old friend, Hakim Moizuddin, in his clinic. The two of them are often engrossed in a discussion of some new medical discovery of Hakim Moizuddin. And, listening to his friend with rapt attention, Deewane Maulvi Sahab imagines that he has all the symptoms of the disease being discussed. "By Allah's grace Moizuddin has found a cure for this disease, or else, I would have died, quite unaware of the cure," he would say to Achhi Begum after getting home. "If you listen to me, Deewane Maulvi Sahab," Achhi Begum reacts sharply, "you should give up the company of this cursed, kalmoonha Hakim of yours. He recounts for you the typical symptoms of every new disease and you get so attracted towards it that you promptly embrace the disease as your mistress and inflict her upon me."

"Arre bhai, he is a very competent Hakim. Your brother too consults him whenever he is in trouble."

"Why would Bhaijaan consult this half-baked Hakim?" Achhi Begum says with a toss of her head. "Take this, I have boiled the water for you. Go on dissolving Moizoo Hakim's medicines in it."

Deewane Maulvi Sahab is in his friend's clinic, saying, "Bhai Hakim Padshah, I don't know why my Begum is always so angry with you."

"Why? I keep giving you rare golden kushte to eat, don't I?"

Their laughter is still rising in their throats when there is a massive explosion near Nawab Mahal. The loud bang seems to have blown out Deewane Maulvi Sahab's senses. At first, Hakim Moizuddin is shocked to see him in this state, and then he begins to examine him closely. And he begins to realize that though before the blast Maulvi Sahab was very much there, he seems to be elsewhere now.

"Maulvi Sahab," Hakim Moizuddin gets up from his seat and goes near him. "Sit down, why have you got up?" Gently pressing his shoulders, he makes Maulvi Sahab sit. "I shall get you some water."

Drinking the water, Deewane Maulvi Sahab comes out of his stupor and says nervously, "My heart is sinking, Hakim Sahab! Something terrible seems to have happened."

"Nothing of the sort, Maulvi Sahab! Just these sains, up to their tricks again today."

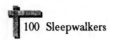

"The blast was heard from over there, wasn't it?" he points towards Nawab Mahal and again gets up with a start.

"Do sit down, Maulvi Sahab! You are getting worried without reason."

Feeling very anxious, Hakim Moizuddin studies his face and, finding the symptoms serious, he begins to get tense. Till now, Deewane Maulvi Sahab himself pulsated in his veins, but now it is only blood that flows in them. Where in heaven has he himself gone? He was mad then, he is mad even now. Though he fully understands the import of the situation, Hakim Moizuddin cannot help the faint smile that flits across his lips. He is Deewane precisely because he is mad through and through.

"Some more water, Deewane Maulvi Sahab?"

"No."

"Then sit down comfortably. These blasts have become part of our everyday life now. In fact, I hear them more when they are not actually taking place." Finding Deewane Maulvi Sahab physically incapable of laughter, Hakim Moizuddin laughs on his behalf also.

"Arre, why don't you sit down? In a short while, we will know how many more were killed today."

"No, I will take your leave now."

But it is as though Deewane Maulvi Sahab has taken leave of himself, not of Hakim Moizuddin. Coming out of the clinic, he takes quick yet heavy strides as if he were walking into the wind and was being pushed back by it.

He feels a twinge of apprehension, wondering whether the blast has occurred in Nawab Mahal itself. Allah forbid, but if this had actually happened, then the whole roof of the Mahal would have crashed down all at once. But Deewane Maulvi Sahab sees the

Mahal falling brick by brick, over and over again, and he rushes home, striding frantically. At one point he almost gets run over by a car. A little further he bumps into a burqa-clad woman. "The road to hell is on the other side, old man," comes a sharp barb from behind the veil. "Why are you coming this way?"

Deewane Maulvi Sahab is not able to comprehend anything. Coming into the vicinity of Nawab Mahal, he has lost all his wits and – Allah have pity – not being able to believe what he sees from a distance, he strains his eyes again and again. His house is surrounded by hordes of people.

Twelve

The bomb that exploded in the garden at the back of Nawab Mahal was so powerful that some people said it had exploded here in Ameenabad, while others said it was in Nazirabad and still others said it was in Maamun ki Qabr. All the Lukhnow-walas felt it had exploded somewhere close to them. The whole city was thrown into turmoil.

Those who died in the blast were naturally no longer there to tell us anything. Of the entire family, only a son and a daughter of Nawab Mirza survived. As did Sain Baba. The boy and the girl were playing hide and seek some distance away in the garden. How were they to know that their parents too would participate in their game and hide in such a way that they would never be found. Sain Baba survived because, at the time of the accident, he had gone to water the plants in the kitchen garden. "Thanedar Sain, before going to the garden, I went to Nawab Sain's room to serve him tea. He was not feeling well ... aa ... so, after lunch he called the factory and told them that he would be resting. He was lying in bed with Chhoti Bibi Sain massaging his head and in the adjoining bed, little Suraiya Sain had just fallen asleep, tired after playing. After serving him tea, I came running to Badi Bibi Sain's room to ask her ... aa ... if she wanted anything. Usually, she sleeps for about half an hour or so after her lunch but today I found her ... aa ... kneeling in prayer. I don't know what it was, Sain, that she was asking for ... aa ... from Allah, making a cup with both her palms, perhaps begging for relief from the pain in her knees ... aa ...! After saying Aameen I turned back quickly to go and quench the thirst of the vegetables ..."

The Inspector interrupted him, "What were you doing at the time of the explosion?"

"This is what I was telling you, Thanedar Sain! I was quenching the thirst of the plants there and here it went off, dha ... dham. I stood up, shocked, and what do I see ... aa ... that the entire back portion of our beautiful Mahal has come crumbling down and in the rubble, buried alive, were our Badi Bibi Sain, Chhoti Bibi Sain, Nawab Sain and ... our shehzadi Suraiya ... aa ... aa ... h ..."

"Where were baba-log at that time?" The Inspector was a Bengali.

"Baba-log?" Sain Baba could not understand. "I am the only baba-log here ... aa ... and I was trembling in terror. Where could I go ... aa .. h ...?"

"No, the children. I mean the boy and the girl."

"Our shehzada Salim and shehzadi Dilnawaz were clinging to each other just a little distance away from me ... aa ... their game forgotten. And do you know what I saw? The children were not aware of it, but a black cobra was swaying near their feet with its hood spread out to protect then. ... aa ... Thanedar Sain, even the black serpent took upon itself the responsibility of protecting these innocents ... aa ... Then why did Allah Mian not save them from becoming orphans?"

After the continuous interrogation over several days, the police came to the conclusion that the culprits had entered the garden by scaling the wall at the back of Nawab Mahal and, after planting the bombs below the jasmine shrubs near the rear building of the mansion, had run away. And what followed after that was bound to happen.

Returning from Hakim Moizuddin's clinic, Deewane Maulvi Sahab tore through the crowds milling around Nawab Mahal and entered the mansion. But, all those who could ease his grief had instead become the cause of his grief and had departed from the world. His Achhi Begum and Nawab Beta and Chand Bahu and his beloved Suraiya lay buried in the tomb of rubble. And, instead of his own people it was an alien – his cook, whose kinsmen had caused this havoc – who was reaching out to him to comfort him. When there is no one else, even an enemy who extends sympathy appears to be a dear one and one feels relieved after crying unabashedly on his shoulders. So Deewane Maulvi Sahab impulsively rushed to Sain Baba, clung to his chest and broke down. He cried and he cried, so much that his sanity was restored.

Thirteen

As soon as he regained his sanity, Deewane Maulvi Sahab realized that he was in Karachi and not in Lucknow, which of course means, he had been in Karachi only since he became normal. Yet now his madness had taken a different turn. Now he innocently believed that he had been living in Lucknow all this while and had come to Karachi only recently on a short visit. He believed Achhi Begum would not let him come, Nawab Mirza and Chand Bibi were not happy with his departure, and his dear grand-daughter Suraiya – Surri – had virtually stopped him with her little arms outstretched, "Bade Abbu, I shall also come with you."

"No, Surri bitiya, don't insist."

"You are taking Bhai and Baji with you, then why not me?"

"Your Bhai and Baji are grown up, bitiya. When you, too, are older ... "

"No, Bade Abbu!"

"Now don't be stubborn, Surri. I shall go and come back very soon!"

Deewane Maulvi Sahab had decided many times that he should get back to Lucknow immediately. Achhi Begum would be getting his paan ready at the proper time every day ... Arre, come back soon, Deewane Maulvi Sahab. What if I also go mad like you? Who will take care of you then?

Thinking of Achhi Begum, his eyes would get wet. Why do you worry about me, Achhi Begum? I feel that you are here with me all the time.

He kept reminding himself that he should go back soon. During those months, Hakim Sahab had come a number of times to Nawab Mahal from Malihabad to counsel Deewane Maulvi Sahab but seeing the mental state of his lunatic brother-in-law, he was unable to muster the courage to speak to him frankly, and could not conceal his tears.

"Hakim Sahab, why do you weep, Bhai? I shall come again." At such moments, Deewane Maulvi Sahab would affectionately squeeze Hakim Sahab's shoulders. "When I come next, I will bring your sister too. What is this foolishness, Nawab Ishaq! You are also crying? All right, all right, I'll bring your Bhaijaan, Bhabhi and Suraiya also. Look, didn't I bring Salim and Dillo this time? They are so happy here that they don't even miss their parents ... Yes, next time I will bring everyone along," he would pat his son

Ishaq Mirza on his back. "Next time, we will all stay here together for as long as you wish. No, Chhote Nawab, don't you worry about me. Your brother and sister-in-law take special care of me and your Ammi ... In fact, they are very indulgent. They are so well-meaning and obedient. May Allah grant them ..." Ishaq Mirza thinks that Deewane Abba will perhaps complete his sentence with "May Allah grant them peace!" but he quickly goes on to say, "May Allah grant them the life of Khizr!"

A month ago, Ishaq Mirza had shifted there from Sindhi Colony with his family. Salma, his Sindhi wife, took the two orphan children under her protection, spreading her soft white wings over them, and entrusted her own Anwar, Jalil and Suveda to the care of their father. Playing and squabbling freely in Salma Begum's lap, Salim and Dilnawaz had, on their own, started calling her Ammi, and Salma Begum never tired of making every effort to nourish this innocent sentiment of theirs. "Ammi, Ammi!" Kissing her face, the four year old Dillo often says to her, "When our Ammi comes back, we will tell her that she is not our ammi. Ammi is our ammi! Isn't it, Ammi?" She kisses her face again. "Ammi, when will our ammi come back? When will Abba come back to us, Ammi?" Listening to the innocent prattle of the little child, Salma and Ishaq, his maternal uncle and aunt and their six sons and their wives and neighbours are all overcome. At such moments, Deewane Maulvi Sahab reaches out and takes her in his arms, "Dillo Beta, we will soon be getting back to your ammi and abba. In just one or two days!" But she says, "No, we will not go to our ammi. Sabi's ammi is our ammi, Bade Abbu."

Khizr: He is believed to ba an immortal saint.

Deewane Maulvi Sahab always kept his own bags and the children's packed and ready. And, every day, rather than take his clothes out of the almirah, he took them out of the suitcase to wear them. He had instructed Salma to get the dirty clothes washed quickly so that he could pack them back, saying, "Now I must get back home!"

"But Abbu," Ishaq Mirza found it difficult to hold himself from blurting out, "Why don't you understand that Ammijaan, Bhaijaan, Chand Bhabhi and Surri, all of them have gone to Allah?"

"No ifs and buts, Ishaq Mian! May Allah bless you. I have seen your Karachi to my heart's content. I am homesick now. Send me back to my Lucknow. If possible, today itself, in fact, just now, beta!"

The river Gomati flooded Ishaq's eyes. Embracing his insane father, he cried out, "Abbujaan ... my dearest Abbujaan, I desperately need you! For God's sake, don't talk of going away, at least not just now."

Deewane Maulvi Sahab opened his mouth to give him a reply but Ishaq placed his hand over his lips. "Please, for the sake of my life!"

After a few days, Maulvi Sahab is once again taken over by his obsession to go back that very day and he is adamant about his departure. Determined to leave, he has neatly arranged all his clothes in his suitcase, tied up his bedding firmly and asked his daughter-in-law to get both the children's bags ready and sent to his room. Meanwhile, playing with a ball, Salim happens to pass through the drawing room. Maulvi Sahab stops Salim, and tells him, "Get ready, Beta, we are going today."

"Going where, Bade Abbu?"

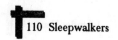

"To Lucknow, Beta! To *our* Lucknow."

Salim fails to understand which Lucknow his Bade Abbu is talking about. He again starts playing with the ball which suddenly bounces out of the room. Chasing the ball, he runs away, saying, "But *this* is Lucknow, Bade Abbu!"

This novella has been translated from a Devanagari transcription of the original Urdu text.

On Writing Sleepwalkers

Joginder Paul

On a visit to Karachi in the mid-eighties, I found I had come to a wonderland. All its people were walking, talking, or whatever, in deep sleep. What was most amazing was that the wonderland looked very familiar! There were so many Uttar Pradesh towns there, situated, I felt, even in the same geographical dimensions. As for the people – they spoke the chaste Urdu that reminds one of pre-Partition days when it was spoken more for aesthetic pleasure than for communicating with people. I would often turn to look questioningly at my host, Muhammad Ali Siddiqui, a fellow-writer in Urdu. The literary critic in him would shrug his shoulders and say, "Well, I would be grateful if *you* could explain our melodrama to me."

Ali is, in fact, the original of Ishaq Mirza, whom I conceived before any other character in *Khwabrau* (Sleepwalkers) and whose forthright bearing provided me with the ending of the novel to work out the beginning from. I found Ali completely involved, like Ishaq, in the here and now, unlike most other mohajirs of Karachi who cannot live their present except in the past tense.

Ali took me to Amroha, Gorakhpur, Meerut, even Malihabad. You won't believe what followed. Before he ventured to take me into the thick of Karachi, he abruptly stopped and said with a gleeful sneer, "From here we shall go forth and witness the grandeur of our great Lucknow ..."

As in India, so in Karachi. The scene led us into the same stationary hubbub of Ameenabad of Lucknow. Roads come here, leisurely sauntering in from numerous directions, each with its cap tipped slightly on one side of the head. And, just as they spot one another at the Chowk, they push themselves forward to get permanently frozen in an embrace. The immense Chowk presents the same clusters of poori-bhajiwalas, kababwalas, mithaiwalas. And, when you have had a bellyful of these delicacies, a light-footed itrawala will approach you respectfully from nobody knows where. Ali eyed me, enjoying my disbelief. "Your whole Lucknow has walked away here into our Karachi, hasn't it? I wonder what's left there."

"The Punjabis," I told him, "who insist on speaking their Urdu in Punjabi!"

Once, well past midnight, Ali and I happened to visit a restaurant in the Lucknow of the mohajirs. The restaurant was as astir with activity then as it must be in its peak hours. My friend remarked that "Lukhnavis" were in the habit of walking out of their dreams at night to come straight to the Chowk. He assured me that these sleepwalkers would keep popping in till the small hours. *Khwabrau* was thus born in my mind. And, months later, when it became ripe for delivery, I prepared myself for what I knew would be a hassle-free labour.

People ask, Why did the mohajirs forsake their homes in India to migrate to Karachi?

And, why, when your home is on fire, don't you flee it to go wherever? Isn't this also how millions of Punjabis, who habitually knew a Hindustani to be one from outside Punjab, suddenly woke up from a nightmare to find themselves in Hindustan. A short story of mine, "Panaahgah" (The Shelter) seeks to depict how post-Partition communal clashes cast their shadows as far as today. In the story, middle-aged Mirasen is the only Muslim inhabitant left behind in her village in Hindustani Punjab after a terrible communal riot. She is disgraced, beaten, repeatedly raped. The poor ignorant woman does not even know where all of her kinspeople have gone. "Why, we have packed them off to Pakistan!" her erstwhile non-Muslim friends jeer. "Why don't you follow them too?" Her kith and kin have actually been temporarily moved to a refugee camp in a neighbouring town. Mirasen is one day found, unconscious with fever and fatigue, by the kindly Sarpanch who then takes her in his bullock-cart to the camp. In the last lines of the story, when she opens her eyes late in the evening in the pale electric light, a young Hindu doctor of the camp affectionately asks her how she is. "Don't be scared, ma," he adds softly, "you have arrived safely." The illiterate Mirasen, moved by his care and kindness, says, "Please inform my people I have reached Pakistan too."

The fact of the matter is that the migrants from India moved – wherever, whenever they did – to "Pakistan," or "the sacred refuge." But it should be interesting to note that Nawab Mirza's wife in *Khwabrau*, for instance, has fearful associations with the word "Pakistan" because of her circumstances. She is scared that her husband has to pass through "a Pakistani corridor" every day on his way to and from work. So, while, Mirasen is happy to have reached her Pakistan while still in India, Achhi Begum is apprehensive of a "Pakistani corridor" in her "Lucknow" in Karachi. The problem cannot, as we realize when we consider it in all its complexity, be resolved with a few impassioned strokes. Here I should perhaps also draw your attention in *Khwabrau* to Sain Baba, a native of Sindh. His poverty has made him a perfect refugee, running from town to town in his own land, in search of his Pakistan. Deewane Maulvi Sahab pities the Sindhi Sain, believing in a rush of pure and plain madness that Sain has had to travel all the way from his native Sindh to their Lucknow for mere food and shelter. So, as it is, the problem is intricate enough and can be solved only with compassionate understanding.

Deewane Maulvi Sahab's emphatic belief that he has been continuously living in his old Lucknow all these years is perhaps pathetic, yet if this belief alone can serve as a divine cure for his malady, why shouldn't we grant him the privilege of madness? But, when a sudden bomb-explosion at Nawab Mahal takes away the lives of his wife, his eldest son and daughter-in-law, you find that the madman is no longer mad. He weeps bitterly on the shoulders of his Sindhi cook and comes out of his madness to suddenly discover, after all these years, that he is, in fact, in Karachi. However, as we soon come to realize, it is only the nature of his madness that has changed. Now he believes that he is in Karachi to visit his son, Ishaq Mirza, and that he must hasten back to Achhi Begum in Lucknow.

Ishaq Mirza, his younger son, has always been aware of the trick that contemporary history has played with the mohajirs. He knows too well the reality of the myth of the Indian Lucknow in Karachi. And, even though affection makes him indulgent towards the belief of his father, he is of the firm opinion that the Lucknow of Karachi can never be dragged back to its Indian origin. Or, that the children who grow up here will have to suffer another mohajirat. Which is why, when Deewane Maulvi Sahab asks his grandson, Salim, to get ready to go back to Lucknow, the lad, running after his ball, answers, "But *this* is Lucknow, Bade Abbu!"

I feel tempted to give a brief account of the situation. For, the situation itself is the meaning that inspired me to attempt the novella. I dedicated it to my friend Muhammad Ali Siddiqui not merely as a gesture, but because he provided me with my favourite character in the novel, Ishaq Mirza. Ali loves his Amroha in India, but would rather live in the Amroha of his children in Karachi, for they know no Indian Amroha except in their grandmother's tales.

Another friend, Anwar Sadeed, an eminent Urdu critic, has always wondered why *Khwabrau* was not written by a Pakistani. But then, isn't it natural that an Indian survivor of the tragic events of the history captured in the novel should also be able to reproduce the anguish of the migrant sensibility and experience?

Like my Deewane Maulvi Sahab, I too had to flee my native land – Sialkot in Pakistan – during the din of the Partition. True, unlike the old man, I was then in my early twenties. Yet, as a child of very simple unschooled old parents, I felt I had suddenly turned grey while taking charge of our dire circumstances, beyond the borders in distant Bharat with which we were familiar only through the slogans and speeches of political bigwigs. Suffer I did no less than Deewane Maulvi Sahab, the suffering having driven the old man out of his wits, and me to an insane pursuit of premature sanity. Anyone rooted securely for generations in the old country named anew, could not have been in more sympathetic concord with migrant life than me. Muhammad Ali Siddiqui once took me to a thickly-peopled wayside in Karachi and pointed to a gigantically calligraphed MOHAJIR on a board as huge as the whole plaza where it had been fixed. I realized what he meant and, voluntarily associating it with my own Indian experience, I turned away rather madly.

I am reminded of another incident which supports my argument. A German Indologist visited me with her husband about the time I had just completed the novella. Reading a few pages of the manuscript while I had been busy talking to her husband, she suddenly let out what sounded like a sob.

"Why ...?" Alarmed, I asked her in my most persuasive voice.

"But this is *my* story," the tear-stricken lady controlled herself to speak. "This is the story of all of us living on either side of the Berlin Wall. Let me tell you what happened to our family ..."

I knew for certain that she was not feigning interest. She had indeed gone through the same terrible experience in different circumstances. So, shall I say, it is not always the same events but the same emotional impact of events that accounts for literary authenticity. But for the emotional felicity available to a writer, his writing will, despite possessing absolutely correct factual details, fail to be creatively substantial. I do believe I am no other than Deewane Maulvi Sahab of *Khwabrau* and, living here in India, I did experience every detail of his life in Pakistan. And, in this specific context, therefore, my dear friend Anwar Sadeed should regard me as a fellow-Pakistani.

On Sleepwalkers

Wazir Agha

translated by Naghma Zafir

*J*oginder Paul's *Khwabrau* is a tale of two cities. It is actually a tale of shifting locales, of migration. However it is quite unlike the archetypal stories of migration in which a particular group of people is compelled to leave a given paradise. In such stories the period of exile comes first and is followed by the desire to retrieve the lost paradise – that is, only after "Paradise Lost" comes the turn of "Paradise Regained." Often, the latter never comes to pass. Yet the hope that the lost paradise will surely appear before their eyes one day always survives in the hearts of the people.

In *Khwabrau* the situation is just the

reverse. The class portrayed here is one which at the end of the dark passage of migration opens its eyes to find itself in the paradise it has lost. Actually, in the process of migration and resettlement, these people have transplanted not only the culture of Lucknow but also its houses, galis and mohallas in the soil of Karachi. Therefore, they recover from their nightmarish journey to find themselves flourishing *and* in their own paradise. They feel no sense of loss at all. Their newfound paradise abounds with wonderful characters who are replicas of the inhabitants of Lucknow. Munwa Chowkidar, Azizo the chai-wala, Chand Bibi, Achhi Begum and above all Deewane Maulvi Sahab – all are integral parts of their paradise.

When one migrates to another land, one leaves behind a horde of things which haunt one always and ultimately lead to a sort of nostalgia. Human beings are like plants. When pulled out, some portion of a person's roots remains in the native soil and the memory of the lost roots tortures him or her for years. However, those migrants from Lucknow did not bring a sapling or seeds with them. Instead, they carried with them the entire tree of the culture of Lucknow which they entrusted to the new land. But a tree is a strange being. Whether you plant a seed or a graft, sooner or later it sprouts roots which begin to draw sustenance from their new soil. In Joginder Paul's novella, this development is depicted when Nawab Mirza's son and daughter – Salim and Dillo – begin to consider Ishaq's Sindhi wife their mother. The mohajir culture gets linked with the local culture and establishes its roots in the new soil. But that happens much later. Most of the

---

This essay was first published in Urdu in *Auraq*, (January-February, 1998), Lahore.

novella deals with the issue of how an imaginary paradise – which exists only in a dream – is mistaken for the real.

The central character of the novel is Deewane Maulvi Sahab, who is mad, but not quite insane. For one is insane when there is a split in one's personality and the two halves of the divided self start growling at each other and create a tension which results in directionless stumbling. Whereas a person like Deewane Maulvi Sahab is well-integrated in his surroundings and has his vision focussed on a beloved, an ideal or some other definite goal, which saves him from being aimless. Deewane Maulvi Sahab is, one should say, an eccentric. The term "deewane" is often used as an endearment for him – but he is definitely not insane. He is so entrenched in his culture that in spite of the fact that he and his family have migrated to Karachi, he does not feel he has moved out of his beloved Lucknow. In a reply to one of Achhi Begum's questions he says, "Where does the question of getting lost arise, Achhi Begum? ... No matter where I go, I can never go out of my own self." This shows that he is perfectly integrated within.

In the novella Deewane Maulvi Sahab regards Karachi as Lucknow. In fact he makes no comparisons between Karachi and Lucknow, for that would require his taking notice of a place which is not Lucknow. He is so absorbed in his Lucknow that he does not take Karachi into cognizance. But Karachi shelters several cultures which gradually begin to enter Maulvi Sahab's cultural Eden – sometimes in the guise of relatives as, for instance, the Sindhi woman Ishaq Mirza gets married to, or in the garb of Sain Baba who takes charge of the kitchen at Nawab Mahal, even in the form of ridicule that Ishaq Mirza levels at the contradictions on the culture of Lucknow. When Hakim Sahab laments the loss of his treasure chest in which he had preserved the documents of the family-tree which described the details of past twenty generations, Ishaq Mirza finds the situation amusing and mockingly comments, "It's only the family-tree the sain fellows have stolen, Mamujaan. Even otherwise, who was going to bother about preserving it after you?" – evidence of how the other culture has penetrated Maulvi Sahab's Eden.

But these infiltrations come stealthily into Maulvi Sahab's paradise. They do not quake the walls of Nawab Mahal but cling on to it as the soft and gentle moonlight. Then one day a violent explosion destroys not only Nawab Mahal, but also buries for ever all those who lived in it. When Nawab Mahal, the centre of Lukhnavi culture falls apart, Maulvi Sahab's personality develops a crack too. As he disintegrates, it is revealed to him that he is actually standing in the middle of two worlds. There is Karachi on one hand, an alien land, as treacherous as Kufa, armed with bombs and Klashnikovs. On the other is Lucknow, steeped in traditions, drenched in love, cherishing age-old cultural values! Suddenly it dawns upon him that he is in Karachi, thousands of miles away from Lucknow and that the city is stifling his breath.

> Deewane Maulvi Sahab realized that he was in Karachi and not in Lucknow, which of course means, he had been in Karachi only since he became normal. Yet now his madness had taken a different turn. Now he innocently believed that he had been living in Lucknow all this while and had come to Karachi only recently on a short visit. He believed Achhi Begum would not let him come, Nawab

Mirza and Chand Bibi were not happy with his departure, and his dear grand-daughter Suraiya – Surri – had virtually stopped him with her little arms outstretched, "Bade Abbu, I shall also come with you."

Now he does not want to stay in Karachi any more. He wants to bid adieu to the city so that he may return to Lucknow immediately.

Determined to leave, he has neatly arranged all his clothes in his suitcase, tied up his bedding firmly and asked his daughter-in-law to get both the children's bags ready and sent to his room. Meanwhile, playing with a ball, Salim happens to pass through the drawing room. Maulvi Sahab stops Salim, and tells him, "Get ready, Beta, we are going today."

"Going where, Bade Abbu?"

"To Lucknow, Beta! To *our* Lucknow."

The bomb explosion has shattered Maulvi Sahab, but it cannot make him part with his paradise. When he finds Karachi closing upon him from all sides, he establishes his lost Eden in the land of his dreams. This exercise saves him from the directionless stumbling of madness. Only, now he is no longer a resident, but a seeker of this lost paradise. The notion of "Paradise Lost" takes a firm hold of him, and in order to retrieve the lost paradise he wishes to return to Lucknow as soon as possible.

This novella which is going to live on presents Joginder Paul as a visionary who with eyes closed has presented such a situation

that people living there have failed to notice even with their eyes
open. It is indeed the skill of a great creative artist which lends
him an insight into reality placed midway between a setting world
and a rising one, between the state of being and that of
nothingness. One is filled with wonder when one finds Joginder
Paul observing this reality so minutely even when he is placed at
such a distance. The well-knit story is a proof of Joginder Paul's
artistic dexterity. Many stories in Urdu written on the theme of
migration usually end in a cul-de-sac. They present situations
where everything is static, but Joginder Paul knows how to keep
his stories open-ended. In *Khwabrau*, when Deewane Maulvi
Sahab's paradise is shattered after being dashed against reality,
he simply picks up the pieces and arranges them in his heart.
Thus a constant process of creating and destroying is taking place
within the story. The story is so skilfully woven that the gaps and
ruptures that appear endow the story with endless possibilities
and dimensions. Viewed from this perspective *Khwabrau* comes
across as an unusual novella in Urdu which has "change" rather
than stasis as its theme. When Deewane Maulvi Sahab is displaced
from Lucknow, he recreates his city in Karachi; and when this
Lucknow crashes down, he finds a place for it in his dreams and
starts preparing for another journey. However he does not shut
himself in this paradise forever. This time he wants to involve
Salim and Dillo too, who actually represent the future. There is
every possibility that he won't let them wander in darkness for
long. In fact, he will bring them back to the world that is changing.
The title of the novel *Khwabrau* itself is a poignant indication
that what is real is the dream and its fluidity. If there are no
dreams there won't be any fulfilment either. The blueprint has

first to appear on the horizon of the mind, only then can it be structured into words, colours, shapes and buildings. Considered from this point of view, Maulvi Sahab is a character who floats on the waves of dreams and is not a paper boat caught in the mire of a dead-end.

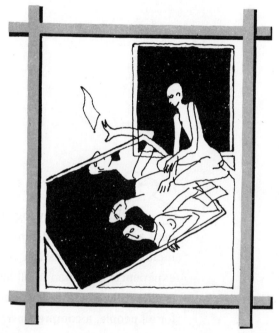

The Art of Joginder Paul

Qamar Rais

translated by Abdul Naseeb Khan

$\mathcal{E}$ach new work by Joginder Paul, be it a novel or a short story, is a new incident, the expression of a fresh experience. Common to all his writing are the feelings of love and compassion for all people, a comprehensive insight into contemporary issues, as well as a grave concern for the sufferings of the masses. Paul easily perceives, explores and comprehends far-reaching cultural and psychological truths in the everyday, ordinary events of life. His is a cosmic vision and every story of his introduces us to a new aesthetic sensibility.

The most widely accepted concept of the short story even today is that it should consist of a new intriguing plot, a dramatic exposition, a startling final twist and some unusual characters. By a harmonious fusion of these elements a writer effectively creates an impressive new work. Most successful and popular stories of all literatures fall in this category, Urdu being no exception. But this traditional concept of the short story has been discarded by many writers, in particular some of the major literary figures of this century. They depend more on a writer's own creative consciousness and aesthetic sensibility. Though careful to retain the spirit of the short story, they have given it a new identity. Joginder Paul is one such celebrated writer. About his collection *Khula* (The Open), he writes:

> I have suffered every one of my stories. I have experienced them in such a way that my characters often appear to be nothing but reflections of my own being. Even when I am no more, I am sure I will remain alive by virtue of my characters. The grain of life is the same, after all. And if it is so, where do people go after they have lived through their own lives? ... I went on slipping naturally into the open so that I may realize the desire of my own life in the lives of others.

Joginder Paul learnt early the art of emerging from troubled waters after many an agonizing experience of swimming, drowning and resurfacing again in this vast sea of life. Towards his characters, his attitude seems to be: I am you, you are me. He has been able to pull apart quickly and easily the veils that usually exist between an artist and life in the early stages of a writer's development.

This essay was first published as "Joginder Paul ka Fanni Asloob" in *Aajkal* (Urdu) in a special issue on Joginder Paul (January 1997).

In the novels and stories that he has written during the last two decades, there is an epiphanic vision of life as a heavy shawl of miseries, disappointments and excruciating loneliness. Any person who dons this shawl acquires his or her own striking and distinctive identity. As Tolstoy has said of families, the happy ones are like one another, but each unhappy family is unhappy in its own way. Only artists, for that matter, are destined to endure agonies and afflictions. And Paul feels this eternal truth with abysmal intensity and faithfulness.

In the preface to the Hindi edition of a collection of his short fiction *Kahan* (Where), he writes:

> How can we imagine life without its trials and tribulations? Once we are born, how can we live on, and for whom, if we don't experience life? How can our stories be born? Whatever they may be – good or bad – by making them actually happen, we become real. It occurs to everyone in the last phase of his life that this journey has all along been futile ... One wonders, Why have I been suffering for so long? But, happiness appears all of a sudden and vanishes in the twinkling of an eye. How long can one live that which is fleeting? Only pain does not go away. It is our sufferings that grant us longevity. If you ever happen to pray for someone's longevity, pray that he may be granted the companionship of sufferings.

Writing stories, delineating characters or bearing afflictions are all the same. The inner logic of the creative process is such that they are inextricably intertwined. His stories are never dictated by any preconceived plot. The motivating factor or the central strain of each story is the awareness of a particular kind of suffering. This then takes the shape of a character who is nurtured within the writer's consciousness for a very long time. His own insight and sensibility shape and perfect the plots. Somewhere Paul refers to the story teller as a maker of toys who collects clay and whose fingers transfer the heat of life into a handful of clay. The toy-maker's hands are like the mother's womb which bring the lifeless to life.

Let us consider some of Paul's recent stories: "Daadiyan" (Grandmothers), "Harikeertan" (Hymn to God), "Chor Sipahi" (Thief and Soldier), "Aage Peechhe" (Front and Back), and "Rone-Dhone ka Sukh" (Bliss of Mourning). Their structural unity is not dependent on an externally projected plot. They are extensions of Paul's own inner "self." In "Daadiyan" the delineation of the grandmother is immortal. A charming representative of the traditions and ethos of Punjab, she faces the agonizing pain of loneliness by recalling thoughts of her old friends. Ensconced in the cradle of her memories, she lives all by herself.

In "Harikeertan" the eldest daughter-in-law suffers greatly at her oppressive and suspicious husband's hands. She remains childless and her dreams are all lost in the dark. She reorganizes her fragmented self with the help of Harikeertan. And, the little boy of "Chor Sipahi" is born and brought up on the footpath. He is in the clutches of a local ruffian, yet he dreams: One day I'll study in a school, have my own bedroom to sleep in and eat to my heart's content. His sunny daydreams prompt him to request a policeman to put him in a jail for juvenile delinquents. But the hawaldar demands a price and says, "First steal something substantial and bring it stealthily to me." Thus an innocent citizen is driven to crime for the sake of some very ordinary dreams. The story ends on an intriguingly poignant note.

"Aage Peechhe" presents a more tragic picture of this kind of misery – very effectively through a single character. In many of Paul's stories the maladies of old age and loneliness emerge as the major problems for humankind in this industrial age. The governments of developed countries and organizations for social welfare are responding to these problems, but in India they go unheeded by intellectuals and government officials. Paul has bitterly felt the sting of this agony. In "Aage Peechhe" one of the characters says:

> In the middle of my field there is an old tree ... It has withered. In its lifetime it must have enjoyed the company of both the living and the dead. It must have burgeoned with life once, but as soon as it grew old it lost its importance. With the passing of the years it grew pale, dry and finally snapped from its inner self.

This is an eloquent allegory of the journey of human life. Always restless to share his treasure of thoughts with others, Paul can use only words and images to do so. They are inseparably linked and complementary to each other. Paul attempts to strengthen words in order to highlight new aspects of life with reference to relationships and human nature. Which is why he doesn't much care for the traditional plot-centred concept of writing stories. The attitude of his characters, their dilemma – the process of delineating which reveals their external and internal "selves" – shape the story.

His multi-layered technique has brought forth a new concept of story-telling. Another development is evident in these stories. Through monologue and address, the writer opts for the literary style of long dialogues in stories like "Utaar" and "Ai Malik." In "Utaar" an old man bares his heart and soul. Wine renders his hold on his consciousness ineffective, but it is through this process that his subconscious starts working and takes the form of confession. Addressing his wife Subhadra, he reveals one by one the secrets of his private and married life. Though the plot is loose, the story contains strong and arresting characters. The husband delves deep into the psychological truths hidden behind their relationship, which he examines ruthlessly.

> What I have learnt from your dark bedroom is nothing but to flaunt my flamboyant lust. No, you are not my wife ... nor am I your husband. Neither are you your real self, nor am I. Under the guise of our names, we are some other people. It is just that legal contract that binds us together. Only the law books maintain our relationship.

In his stories Paul uses metaphors more often than symbols. Symbols have various meanings. They don't present perfect pictures of social and cultural situations. Metaphors unravel the secrets of human life by drawing comparisons between nature or other elements of the world and human life. Let's take "Gaadi." It deals with a middle-class small family's journey by train. From the exposition to the conclusion, the writer maintains a balance between realism and fiction. The first person narrator talks, in a simple fashion, of the difficulties the passengers encounter during the journey and forces the reader to feel that these events are indicators of some established and complex order. The narrator is an honest retired officer of the Department of Education. He values his honesty, civility and goodness above all else. But during this journey, railway officials, some policemen and officials of the Excise Department treat him like a criminal. Reserved seats are occupied unlawfully. The railway staff do not solve the problems of the passengers; on the contrary they foment them and amuse themselves. At a station some Excise officers, along with policemen, enter the compartment. One of them asks the narrator with a smile "How much medicine are you carrying?" Dumbfounded the narrator says, "I am not carrying any."

> "Yes, what else except opium can you take from here?" they say.
> "I am a decent man. Don't talk like this."
> "Only gentlemen do this business," the policeman with the gun speaks. "Search his bags."
> "This is high-handedness. I have nothing illegal on me."
> "But we can recover opium from your bags even if they have nothing in them."

The narrator is terror-stricken. To his good fortune he hears the whistle of the train blow and it begins to move. Such ups and downs impart a sense of wonder and interest to the story. Mansho, the narrator's grandson, adds new meaning to the events with his curiosity.

> "Bam! Bam, the train is reversing," the child asks his grandfather.

"Oh yes, it is really reversing raji."

Someone shouts from the next compartment,
"Why is the train reversing?"

"The bridge ahead is broken."

The train goes on reversing. Here, the train is a metaphor for time and the reader finally discovers the great analogy between the journey of an individual's life and that of the society to which he belongs. This journey leads us, in the name of progress and development, towards the caves of the past where man, in spite of being wild, was not as oppressive, selfish, malicious, hypocritical and scheming as he is found to be at the end of this journey. He has fallen prey to terror, insecurity and fear psychosis.

"Khodu Baba Ka Makbara" (Khodu Baba's Tomb) narrates the story of a stray dog. The entire story develops through mysterious symbolism. About the people who lie buried in a graveyard, this story could be described as "a symbolic allegory." Fakir Khodu Baba finds a raised platform on one corner of the graveyard. Impressed with his saintly bearing, Chowdhary, the contractor of the graveyard builds Baba a shelter. After that, people of both the graveyard and the huts by its side come to visit him and listen to his preachings. These afflicted transgressors and disappointed people begin to develop staunch faith in Baba, who emerges here as a symbol of truth, virtue and generosity. Paul didn't lose his poise in drawing a half-bright picture of the mysterious valley of the shadows in this narrative. The dramatic revelation in the story takes place at the juncture when the readers discover that Baba himself is the son of the dog whose story he is narrating. As a young man says, "Baba, shall I say it? *You* are the son of the dog."

Some people complain that there is a kind of monotony in the themes and techniques found in the stories of Joginder Paul. In many stories where he has a first person narrator, Paul has made use of a kind of internal soliloquy. This treatment creates the impression that his themes are the same, but it is not so. Paul's stories, though simply written, are suggestive and each of them varies thematically. His characteristically subtle play of theme and narrative technique is evident in a story like "Bujhte Suraj Ka Samay" (The Time of the Setting Sun), a recent masterpiece of Urdu short fiction.

The resources by which Paul maintains creative unity bear testimony to his grasp over his themes. It is necessary to stress here that his use of language is extremely sensitive. It is impossible to identify his art without understanding this aspect of his writing. So far as styles in Urdu stories and novels are concerned, Krishan Chander, Manto and Ismat Chugtai seem to have influenced most writers. But Paul's style has its own distinct identity. His technique is inimitable, shaped as it is by his life and personal experiences. Undoubtedly, the stories of Joginder Paul are the culmination of artistic maturity and excellence.

On

"The Goatherd" & *"A Palace in Paradise"*

Joginder Paul

I was asked to choose two Urdu short stories, one by a writer of an earlier generation and the other representing the generation at my heels. Although I regard enduring writers of all generations as contemporaries, I was rather intrigued by the proposal. I thought that the process of choosing might help me perceive more vividly the difference in communal responses to the quality of life in our times and in recent history. I have been seriously engaged with this issue for some time. The two excellent stories that I selected for this volume seek to unravel two astonishingly dissimilar responses to the same theme, religious morality. In "Gadaria" (The

Goatherd) by the old-timer Ashfaque Ahmad, an incredibly simple
and learned Hindu wears his faith in Islam as he does his spotless
skin. In Sajid Rashid's "Jannat Mein Mahal" (A Palace in Paradise)
a well-meaning young Muslim wears this faith too, but as his
immaculate dress, and is scared that someone may suddenly tear
it open to discover the spots on his skin.

The heyday of the Progressive Movement in Urdu literature
lasted comfortably till the advent of Independence. At their best
the Progressives indeed broke new ground both in the treatment
and choice of subjects, but at their worst, which was enough to
wreak havoc, they unashamedly dubbed a creative writer a pariah
if he did not appear to tow their line as enunciated – barely! – in
the manifesto of the Communist Party of India. The political
credentials of Ashfaque Ahmad not being acceptable to the Party,
"Gadaria" had to lie in the dustbin for about a decade till the sky
was cleared of this binding ideology and readers could make bold
to evaluate literary writing in its own specific creative contexts. It
is heartening to note that, upon its discovery, "Gadaria" was
universally acknowledged as a minor classic, perfect in its
proportions.

A very humble middle-aged Hindu devotee of Islamic thought
and culture, Dauji is a poor village court scribe who never awaits
or approaches a client to earn his living. He has this clumsy choti,
a tuft of hair allowed to grow unhampered at the centre of the
head as a mark of his ancestral dharma, and he often recalls how
his mother used to wash the choti with curd, after which she combed
and stroked it gently with her fingers. Every once in a while Dauji
feels the presence of his late murshid (teacher and mentor) Hazrat
Maulana and, on such occasions, he recites the Islamic teachings

of the master in devout gratitude, unmindful of his choti slipping out from under the folds of his massive turban. Then, suddenly thinking of his unwilling young pupil, he turns to solving Geometry propositions for him. The unwilling student's father, a Muslim munsif at the court has handed the boy to Dauji as a day-and-night charge. Does Dauji receive a fee, big or small, for the arduous duty? No! he does it out of love for the unruly boy, and even more, for dutifully spreading the light in the tradition of his Hazrat Maulana.

Dauji recounts how he would have remained an unlettered goatherd all his life but for Hazrat Maulana's pious interest in him. The Hazrat schooled him in the finest human values through Persian and Arabic texts of philosophy and science. But even after becoming a full Chintaram from a mere Chintu and consequently a fuller Dauji, he never forgets his original calling. He continues to tend even the wildest of human goats as part of his own herd. Thus, towards the end of the story, when Rano, a fellow goatherd from his earlier days and a Muslim scoundrel, picks on him during a 1947 communal riot and, having got his choti almost pulled out with a blunt weapon, orders him to read the Kalma, the disciple of the Hazrat regards the ignorance of the street rascal compassionately and inquires calmly, "Which one?" The story here takes a masterly turn to end at the beginning. Rano pushes the staff of the goatherd into Dauji's hand and commands him to lead his herd into the neighbouring jungle as he did in his early days. And, "Unturbanned, Dauji started walking behind the goats, like a long-haired Baba Farid."

Religion in the good old days was the mainspring of unconscious moral activity. Today, in an amoral environment, it is a hideout to priggishly peep out from. Sajid Rashid's Mushtaque in the superb "Jannat Mein Mahal" typifies the contemporary man who sports a beard to claim social legitimacy as a Mussalman. Mushtaque is forced to be a young hustler who, for the sake of the company's business, arranges pretty women for potbellied Arab and African customers. He is, of course, disapproving of his unethical acts on principle and perhaps waits for a convenient time or a suitable action to discontinue them. But the reader is made to realize that this go-getter is unlikely to ever withdraw from his everyday profane professional activities unless perhaps the day when he succeeds the Managing Director of the company from whom he now takes orders which he follows slavishly. And why should he not? If Mushtaque decides to go by the retarding scruples of conscience, where will the money to hold his head up as a proper Mussalman come from? The eyes of his god-fearing old father, from whose virtuous living he draws inspiration to adhere to the cause of Allah, have to be operated upon. The operation will incur a lot of expenditure, but it matters little as long as his company is happy with him. Besides, he can buy, in a moment, a whole book of twenty-five receipts of twenty-five rupees each and thus contribute significantly in the sacred duty of building the extension of the village masjid and madrasa. His religious father has always forbidden him from doing ungodly deeds. Yet, how else can the Palace in Paradise be built? Not only this, he has also to help his father acquit himself of the duty of the marriage of Guddi, his sister and playmate of their innocent childhood. So much of the pure good he chooses to do depends entirely upon his capacity to keep the devil smiling. So, for the time being, it's enough that he sincerely and regularly "reads" the Darud-sharif from memory where his infirm father has firmly imprinted it. The brilliant rendering of Mushtaque's moral and religious predicament goes on mounting steadily and develops into an unpleasant situation in which the poor young man is constrained to pursue his religion with a commercial and "secular" conscience. And, in the process, you suddenly find yourself counting the times when you were likewise forced to play Mushtaque. The quiet way in which the story encroaches upon your own life is worth experiencing.

The stuff that constitutes most contemporary Indian short stories is often made of a helpless and heavy accounting direct from the writers to justify their viewpoints. We cannot but feel in both these stories a natural rotundity of action which makes them roll inevitably on their own slopes. It is, in fact, this feeling of inevitability of a movement in a story which disturbs and modifies the consciousness of its reader and makes him or her hold on to it for long.

I am indeed pleased to invite my readers to read through these "large" specimens of short fiction, so different in meaning and approach, yet so similarly occupied with the truth of religion at its core.

The Goatherd

Ashfaque Ahmad
translated by Ameena K Ansari

It was a long, freezing winter night. I was fast asleep, huddled in my razai, when I was rudely awakened.

"Who is it?" I shouted.

A large human hand brushed against my head and, in the dark, a voice answered, "The police have arrested Rano."

"What?" I tried to push away the trembling hand. "What is it?"

Again the voice wafted across the darkness, "The police have arrested Rano. Translate this into Persian."

"Dauji!" I said in a tearful voice. "You always disturb me in the middle of the night. Go away! I don't want to stay in your house and I don't want to study!" I burst into tears.

Dauji now spoke in an affectionate tone, "How do you expect to pass the examination if you don't study? And if you don't pass how will you become a successful man? How will people get to know about your Dauji?"

"May Allah's wrath fall on everyone ... On you, your friends ... and me." The thought of dying young brought on hiccups and more tears.

Dauji patted my head reassuringly and said, "That's enough. Stop crying, Beta. Just translate this one sentence and I will not disturb your sleep again."

As tears rolled down my face, I retorted angrily, "Today the bastards have arrested Rano; tomorrow they will take away someone else. Your translation ..."

"No, no!" he cut in. "After this I promise never to disturb you while you are sleeping. Come on, translate: *The police have arrested Rano.*"

"I can't do it," I replied peevishly.

"One must not give up so easily," Dauji coaxed. "Try once again."

"I won't," I said stubbornly.

A faint smile flickered on his face as he said, "Karkunan-e-gazmah-khana Rano tauqueef kardand. Karkunan-e-gazmah-khana means the police. Don't forget that – it's an unfamiliar word and a new grammatical structure. Now memorize it by repeating it ten times."

I knew I could not easily escape the determined Dauji, so I did as I was told. When I had said the same thing ten times, Dauji

---

This story was first published in Urdu as "Gadaria" in *Ujle Phool* (1957), a collection of the author's short fiction.

interrupted once again, "Now repeat the whole sentence five times." I did. Then, drawing the razai over me, he warned, "Don't forget it. I'll test you in the morning."

Then he withdrew.

In the evenings, after finishing my Quran lessons with Mullahji, I usually walked home through the kharasi gali. Though I met a number of people on the way, I was acquainted only with a fat man who was the bhishti. My friends made fun of this water carrier by calling him, "Kaddu-karela dhai anna." Next to his house was an enclosure for goats, bound on three sides by mud-plastered houses. Facing these houses was a patch of wild, thorny bushes, next to which lay an open field. Adjoining this was the one-room tenement of the lame blacksmith. His walls touched a brick-layered house that had saffron-coloured windows and an impressive door studded with brass nails. At this point the gali took an imperceptible turn and became narrow, so narrow that as one walked along, it seemed to brush against one's shoulders. It was perhaps the longest, and the most deserted gali in our little town. Whenever I passed through it, I felt as if I was walking down the barrel of a gun and a bullet would go through me as soon as I emerged from its oppressive mouth. In the evenings, however, I always met others walking that way and my fears would fade away.

On these walks, I often encountered a tall man with a white moustache. He would be wearing a muslin turban, a long and loose khaki-coloured coat, a khaddar pajama and flat boots. He was often accompanied by a young boy, of about my age. His clothes were similar to the old man's. With his hands in his pockets, his head bent low, the elderly man would be talking in gentle tones. The boy and I would look at each other as we drew abreast and then go our different ways.

As my brother and I were returning home one day, after an unsuccessful fishing expedition at the local pond, we saw this same person sitting on the parapet of a bridge. His turban lay on his lap, exposing his ruffled white hair which stuck to his scalp like the unruly dirty feathers of a hen. As we passed him, my brother raised his hand to his forehead and said, "Dauji, salaam!" His greeting was returned with a nod of the head and "Jeetey raho."

Realizing that this man was known to my brother, I also greeted him in my childlike voice and got the same reply. Bhaiya then slapped me for being too forward and hissed, "You boastful creature ... you dog! Why did you say salaam to him when I had already done so? Why do you interfere in everything I do? Tell me, do you know who he is?"

"That's Dauji," I said, swallowing my tears.

"Don't talk nonsense," snapped Bhaiya, with angry, blazing eyes. "You mimic me all the time, you show-off."

I walked along silently. I was happy to make Dauji's acquaintance and did not bother much about Bhaiya's violent outburst which was a frequent occurrence, anyway. Being older, he was always bullying me.

As I got to know Dauji better, I took to walking through the gali at those times when I knew I would run into him. Greeting him, and then getting his reply, gave me a sense of elation which made me float on air. For a year, our relationship was restricted to this ritualistic greeting.

Meanwhile, I learnt that Dauji lived in the house with the saffron-coloured windows and that the young boy who accompanied him was his son. When I tried to extract more information about them from my brother, I only succeeded in making him angry. Every time I asked him a question, his reply was, "How does that concern you?" or "Don't talk rubbish."

Many questions about Dauji would rise in my mind, but luckily they did not bother me for too long. When I passed the class four examination from Islamia Primary School, I was admitted to class five in M B High School. And then, without having to incur Bhaiya's favour, I discovered that Dauji's son was my classmate and that father and son belonged to the Hindu Khatri community. Dauji earned his livelihood by drafting petitions at the local court. His son, Amichand, was the brightest boy in our class. Amichand always wore a very long turban and had a catlike face. Some boys had nicknamed him "Miaow," others called him "Nevla" – mongoose. I always called him by his name. So we became friends. We exchanged gifts, promising to remain friends forever.

I visited Amichand's house a few days before the summer vacations began. On that hot, scorching afternoon I paid little heed to the pangs of hunger or to the relentless rays of the sun when I accompanied Amichand home from school. I had gone to borrow the absorbing tales of Sheikh Chilli. His home, though small, was spotlessly clean. After passing through the brass-studded door, one came to a little passage which opened out onto a spacious courtyard. Facing this stood a brick-coloured verandah, on one side of which was a large room. In the corner of the courtyard grew a pomegranate tree and some aqeeq bushes. A wide staircase wound its way up from another section of the courtyard and in the space under the stairs was a tiny kitchen. Brick-coloured windows opened towards the sitting room which had blue doors.

As soon as we stepped into the passage, Amichand shouted, "Bebe, namaste," and entered the sitting room, leaving me stranded in the middle of the courtyard. Bebe, sitting on a mat in the verandah, was absorbed in running her sewing machine. The young girl who sat next to her was cutting some dress material. Responding to Amichand, the former mumbled something. The young girl, however, looked up at me and turned to Bebe, saying, "I think it is Doctor Sahab's son."

The whirring sewing machine fell silent.

"Oh yes," smiled Bebe, beckoning to me. Twisting the strings of my jusdan which held the Quran, I walked with faltering steps towards the verandah and leaned against the pillar.

"What is your name?" asked Bebe affectionately and I told her in a whisper, my eyes riveted to the floor.

"He looks just like Aftab, doesn't he?" said the girl, laying down her scissors. "And why not? They are brothers after all."

A voice from within enquired, "Aftab. What is it, Beta Aftab?"

"It's Aftab's brother, Dauji," called the young girl. "He has come with Amichand."

Dauji emerged from the interior of the house. His pajamas were rolled up to his knees and he was without his kurta. His turban was upon his head as always. Holding a small bucket of water, Dauji came to the verandah and, peering at me, remarked, "Yes, there is a striking resemblance, but this one has a rounder face."

Putting down the bucket, he patted my head and sat down on a wooden stool. He then lifted his feet, gently brushed the dust from them, and immersed them in the bucket.

"Does Aftab write home?" he asked me, splashing water on his legs.

"He does," I replied slowly. "We got a letter the day before yesterday."

"What does he say?"

"I don't know. Only my father can tell you."

"Yes," he said, shaking his head, "You should ask him. One who doesn't ask questions never acquires knowledge."

I was silent. After a while Dauji asked, "Which chapter of the Quran are you reading?"

"The fourth," I stated with confidence.

"What is the third chapter called?"

"I don't know," I said, my voice fading away.

"Tilkar Rasool," he replied, taking his hands out of the bucket and shaking them dry.

All this while, Bebe kept running her sewing machine. The young girl brought some food and laid it on the wooden chauki. Amichand was still in the sitting room.

I continued to twist the strings of my jusdan, overcome with shyness. Once again, Dauji, setting his eyes on me, said, "Recite the Surah-e-Fateha."

"I don't know it," I replied, in great embarrassment. He looked at me intently and said, "Can't you even recite the Alhamdo-Lillah?"

"I can recite that," I countered quickly.

He smiled and said softly, "It's the same thing ... the same thing."

Then he nodded to indicate that I should start. As I began, he rolled down his pajamas and spread the open end of his turban across his shoulders. When I came to the end of my recitation, he joined me in saying, "Aameen!"

I expected Dauji to give me some sort of reward, just as my uncle had done when I had recited the same lines for him. Not only had he uttered "Aameen!" with me, he had also given me a rupee. Dauji, however, remained motionless, almost as if he had turned to stone. Just then Amichand came out with the book he was going to lend me. I took leave of Dauji, saying softly, "Dauji salaam" and just as softly he returned, "Jeetey raho." Bebe interrupted her sewing and said, "Come and play with Amichand sometimes."

"Yes, yes, do come," Dauji repeated, in startled tones. "Aftab, too, came here quite often but now he has gone so far away." He then lapsed into some Persian couplets.

This was my first formal encounter with Dauji and I left with the feeling that he was an old miser who used words sparingly and was slightly deaf. Later that day, I told my mother about my visit and mentioned that Dauji still had fond memories of Aftab.

Ammi's voice was bitter as she scolded me, "You should have at least asked me ... I know he has tutored Aftab, who holds him in high esteem. But your Abbaji is not on speaking terms with him. They had a difference of opinion over something a long time ago and the anger still remains. If Abbaji gets to know of your visit he will be furious." Then, in a more sympathetic tone, she continued, "Don't mention this to your Abbaji."

I didn't. But I continued to visit Dauji often. He would be reclining on a mat with some book when I got there. I would tiptoe in and stand behind him, but he always knew when I had entered and, snapping his book shut, he would say, "So Golu, you've come. What news do you bring?"

I would try and answer this question as best as I could and he would be greatly amused. I remember now that though my comments were not very interesting, Dauji always smiled for my sake. Then he would produce a piece of paper from his register and say, "Here, solve this problem."

These problems always seemed too difficult to solve but his encouragement would reassure me. And the problems were interspersed with conversation which made these sessions extremely interesting. Gradually the questions became so involved that they took up all my time. If I managed to answer his questions faster than expected he would finger his mat and ask, "What is this?"

"A mat," I would declare.

"Unh-hunh," he would shake his head. "Say it in Persian."

"Am I taught Persian?"

"I will teach you, Golu. I will tell you now. Listen. It's Boriya in Persian and Hasir in Arabic."

In mock dismay I would entreat, "Not Persian and Arabic together. I don't want to study them ... spare me."

He would ignore all my protests and keep repeating the Persian and Arabic translations. Even if I had sealed my ears with molten wax, it would not have deterred him from this repetition.

Amichand was a bookworm who spent all day in the sitting room, reading or writing. Though Dauji never interfered with his routine, he reviewed Amichand's progress very minutely. Once, when Amichand was drinking water, Dauji asked, "What is the noun form of the word Do?"

Without removing his lips from the glass, Amichand answered, "Deed" and, flinging the glass aside, walked back to his room. Dauji returned to the book he was reading.

Dauji loved his daughter dearly. We all called her Bibi but his special name for her was Qurrah. Often he would ask her, "Beti, when will you lay aside your scissors?"

Bibi would just smile demurely. But her mother, Bebe, would retort, "By giving her that name you have tempted kismat to give her a profession that rhymes with her name. Qurrah, the one who stitches kurtas. I believe that one should have measured speech and use auspicious words that augur well."

Dauji would then take a deep breath and say, "How can an illiterate person understand the true meaning of this word?"

These remarks infuriated Bebe and from her lips issued a stream of abuses. If Bibi intervened, Dauji would remark, "Abuses, like the wind, flow unrestrained. One should not try to curb either of them."

Then he would gather his books and his mat and silently go up the stairs.

In class nine I formed a bad habit which made me do strange things. Ali Ahmad, now dead, was the only hakim in our township. Instead of giving the usual prescriptions, Hakimji believed in curing people with magical tales about godmen, supernatural beings and the domestic lives of King Solomon and Queen Sheba. These worked wonders on his poor, illiterate patients. His dark and dingy clinic boasted of a few jars of potions and powders. Patients would come to him from distant villages and return home feeling cured after his unique methods of therapy.

After a few weeks' acquaintanceship, I struck a deal with Hakimji. I would steal empty jars and bottles for him from my father's hospital and, in return, he would lend me books like *The Saga of Amir Khusrau*. These books were so absorbing that I would be lost in them for several nights and not get up on time. This upset my mother immensely while my father worried about my health. Though I spoke of my intentions of getting a scholarship in class ten, most of my nights were spent in roaming the magical worlds of the books lent to me by Hakimji, and my days, standing on a bench in the classroom, punishment for not being attentive. I almost failed in the quarterly examinations, fell ill in the half-yearly and scraped through the annual examinations with the assistance of Hakimji, who connived with my teachers.

In class ten *Sandali Nama*, *Fasana-e-Azad* and *The Arabian Nights* were my favourite books. The latter lay in my school-desk, while the others were kept at home. Sitting on the last bench in the classroom, I was often lost in the adventurous world of Sindbad, whose story I hid between the pages of my geography book.

At ten in the morning on the twenty-second of May, the class ten results were declared in the school. Amichand had topped not only in our school but in all the other schools in the district. Twenty-two boys had passed and six had failed. Hakimji's influence could not prevail over the university and I was among the six who had failed.

That evening Abbaji thrashed me and threw me out of the house. I spent half the night by the rehett in the hospital, contemplating the future course of action. I was familiar with the daredevilry of Umru Ayyar and Sindbad but these had not equipped me to face life. For a long time I sat like a statue, reviewing the limited options before me. My mother found me in this state and took me back home, promising to seek Abbaji's forgiveness on my behalf. Forgiveness meant nothing to me; all I needed was a good night's rest before I set out on a long journey. So, as was my custom, I stretched out on my bed.

Rehett: A water-drawing device.

The next day I met Khushia, Kodu and Dilsweb – the other boys who had failed – behind the mosque. Dilsweb informed us that Lahore, being a commercial city, was the right place to start a business. He mentioned a relative of his who ran a flourishing business with Fateh Chand, a contractor. Within two years this relative had bought two cars. When I asked him about the nature of the business we could start, Dilsweb brushed aside my question, saying Lahore was the centre of all kinds of trade and all one needed was an office with a signboard outside. When I enquired if a lot of money was required, Kodu brusquely said that Dilsweb had just made these things very clear. Kodu then asked Dilsweb whether the Anarkali Bazaar or the Shah-e-Alami would be a suitable location. I suggested that Anarkali, by figuring prominently in advertisements, would be the appropriate place. It was finally decided that the next day we would all board the two o'clock train to Lahore. On reaching home, I made the necessary preparations for the journey. Just as I was polishing my shoes, the servant came in, smiling cheekily, and announced, "Come quickly. Doctor Sahab wants to see you."

"Where is he?" I said, putting down the shoebrush and standing up.

"In the hospital," he smirked, having been a witness to the thrashing meted out to me.

Filled with dread, I climbed the stairs, opened the door and entered my father's room. Sitting beside my father was Dauji. I greeted him with diffidence and, after a long time, heard his usual blessing, "Jeetey raho."

"Do you recognize him?" asked my father harshly.

"Without doubt," I answered like a civilized salesman.

"You swine, you haraamzade, I know all your ..."

"No, no, Doctor Sahab," Dauji interjected, raising his hands, "He is a very nice young boy who has ... "

Abbaji interrupted in a bitter tone, "You don't know, Munshiji, this swine has trampled my honour to dust."

"Don't worry," reassured Dauji, lowering his head. "He is much brighter than our Aftab and one day ... "

By now Abbaji was incensed and, slapping my hand, he said, "What rubbish, Munshiji! He is not fit to be compared to Aftab."

"He'll be all right, he'll manage, Doctor Sahab," nodded Dauji gravely, "Don't worry."

Then he got up from the chair and, putting his hands on my shoulders, said, "I'm going for a walk. Come with me and we'll talk on the way."

Abbaji fidgeted with his registers and muttered in fury. As I walked slowly towards the latticed door, Dauji turned back and remarked, "Don't forget to send it immediately."

Flinging his things about, Abbaji replied in the affirmative. Dauji bid him good-bye and walked out of the door.

Dauji and I went for a long walk during which he told me the Persian names of many trees we saw on the way. We made our way to that very bridge where I had first made my acquaintance with him. Sitting in his usual place, Dauji put his turban on his lap and, after running his hand over his head, gestured to me to sit in front of him. Then, closing his eyes, he said, "From today I will teach you. Even if you can't top your class, I should certainly be able to help you secure at least a first division. Allah has always helped me in all my endeavours and I have never been disappointed."

"I don't want to study," I declared rudely.

"What else will you do?" he asked with a smile.

"I want to start a business, earn money, buy a car and show everyone ..."

This time Dauji interrupted me and in an affectionate voice, said, "May you possess ten cars! But neither I, nor Doctor Sahab, would ever consent to sit in the car of an illiterate man."

"I don't care about anyone," I snapped. "Doctor Sahab can stay happy in his house and I shall be happy in mine."

Dauji then asked in astonishment, "You don't care for me either?"

I was going to say something when I saw the sadness on his face and heard him repeating, "Not bothered about me, Golu? ... Not even about me?"

I felt sorry when I heard the tone of his voice and I said softly, "I do care about you but ..."

My words went unheard as Dauji said, "Could I have ever dreamt of speaking like this in front of my master? If I had ever uttered such sacrilege then ... then ..."

He placed his turban on his head, and said, "I was an insignificant cur before my master ... perhaps more insignificant than the dust beneath his feet. Being a disciple, I could never speak like this. I would be an accursed man if I had ever done such a thing."

Then, folding his hands across his chest, he bowed his head and continued, "I am a gadaria, a goatherd, by caste. My father was a milkman from Mandasi. I was a child of ignorance, my family, the descendants of Abu Jehel. One benign glance, one little gesture from Aaqa, the Almighty, and the humble Chintu was transformed into Munshi Chintaram. People address me as

Munshiji but I call myself a humble servant of one on whom falls the grace of Allah ... People understand this."

In a trance, he kept kissing his fingertips, and intermittently recited Persian couplets. Confused and embarrassed, I touched his knees and called out his name but the only answer I got was the repetition of, "My master, my mentor, my guide." When this state of absorption weakened, he looked up and said, "What pleasant weather! The intense heat of the day gives way to cool evenings."

Getting up from the parapet of the bridge, he continued, "Let's go and buy some provisions from the bazaar."

The aggression and ill-temper with which I had accompanied Dauji were now replaced by an acute sense of contrition.

From Dilsweb's father's store he purchased the required provisions, which were given to him in a paper bag. I wanted to carry the bag but could not muster enough courage to ask him for it. A strange feeling of hesitation and embarrassment held me back and at last we reached his house. When I saw my bedclothes and hurricane lantern there, I realized that I would now live with Dauji, who would give me lessons.

It was obviously not destined that I rise in business and drive around in a Packard. Those of my friends who made it to Lahore were also brought back by their parents but I knew that had I been there our business venture in Anarkali would have been a stupendous success.

Dauji made life hell for me. He almost destroyed me and I lost my zest for life. The whole day was spent on boring school lessons and the short summer nights passed in answering his questions.

His charpai was placed next to mine on the terrace and he would keep asking me inane questions about things like the waterways of Moong Rasool and Marala. Even if I answered correctly he would repeat the question and I, greatly irritated, would snap back, "I don't know. I won't answer you."

This would silence him. I would shut my eyes to sleep but shame, like a speck of dust, would prick my eyelids, compelling me to whisper, "Dauji."

A sober "Hunh" followed.

"Ask another question," I would say.

"All right," he would reply and proceed to give me a sentence to analyze grammatically.

Humbly I would say, "This is a long sentence. In the morning I'll write it down and then analyze it. Ask me something else now."

Looking up at the sky, Dauji would say, "My Golu is a fine boy."

After a moment, I would say, "That's a good sentence ..."

Dauji would suddenly sit up on his charpai and, raising his hands, say, "Haven't I told you to specify the speaker first?"

I would ask another question to avoid the difficult exercise, "Why do you call me jan-e-pidar? Why not Dauji's beloved boy?"

"Well done!" he would say happily. "Such things are meant to be questioned. Jan is a Persian word for beloved, but Dauji is from Bhasha. One cannot insert a Persian term in between. Those who make frequent use of such speech err greatly."

I then realized that I had become entangled in an issue that was far more convoluted than grammatical structures. I immediately feigned a yawn and told Dauji that I was extremely sleepy. "What about the grammatical structures?" he would quickly say.

Despite all the excuses and deliberate changes in the topic of conversation, Dauji would keep sitting upright on his charpai. If the answer took long in coming, he would put on his turban and wait, making it abundantly clear that he was ready to wait longer for the right answer.

When Amichand left home for college, I not only moved into his room but also came to occupy his place in Dauji's heart. Though I now loved Dauji, I still resented some of his views, perhaps more than before. As I understood human psychology better, I was more sensitive than Dauji. I intensely disliked his habit of shooting questions at me all the time and discouraging me from taking part in games. He wanted one to immerse oneself in books till death came, and surrender to it, surrounded by piles of books. To maintain one's health he believed in taking long walks and, that too, early in the morning. About two hours before dawn, he would come and shake me awake, "Get up, Golu. You've become fat."

Most parents wake their children up by either saying that morning has broken or the sun is out but Dauji would wake me by making insulting references to my size. Whenever I showed resentment, he would lovingly say, "If you become any fatter, how will you ever be able to tour the district on horseback?"

From the warmth of my bed I would, with folded hands, entreat him, "Kill me, but don't wake me up so early."

These words of mine weakened his resolve and he would quickly put the quilt back over me and go away.

Bebe had a long-running feud with Dauji who was quite scared of her. She spent the whole day stitching the neighbours' clothes and cursing Dauji. Bebe's constant nagging made me furious, but one cannot be inimical to the crocodile if one has to survive in his watery domain. Dauji would seek refuge in my room when Bebe took to using particularly vulgar abuses. Putting his hands over his ears, he would remark, "I know it is a sin to talk behind someone's back, but your Bebe is a sharp-tongued bhatiyaran whose influence rubs off on everyone. All three of us are weary travellers on the road of life."

Bebe's looks complemented her temper. She was extremely dark and had flashing white teeth, a wide forehead, and beady eyes. She walked stealthily like a cat and spread vicious gossip wherever she went. She would even drive Bibi to tears with her cutting words. With Amichand, she got on well. Perhaps because they resembled each other or perhaps because he did not adore Dauji like his sister did.

Though poor Bibi was a nice person, I did not get along well with her. Whenever I was on the roof, doing my work, she would come there to get firewood for the chulha. Looking at me, she would peer over the parapet and inform Dauji, "He's not studying, he's making carts out of straw."

Making a face at her I would say, "Why are *you* so bothered if I don't work? Why should you grumble? ... Behaving like a thanedarni!"

Dauji would call out from downstairs, "No, no, Golu, one does not quarrel with one's sister."

I would shout back, "I am studying. She's just telling lies."

Dauji would slowly climb the stairs and, observing my handiwork hidden under the books, say, "Dear Qurrah, don't tease him. I have managed to subdue this djinn after tremendous effort. If he goes astray again I shall have great difficulty restraining him."

Bibi would then request Dauji to pick up my books and see where I had hidden the toy cart. I would glare at her and she would go downstairs with the firewood. Then Dauji would pacify me by saying, "Bibi does this for your good. Else why should she bother to tell me? Whether you pass or fail, she has your welfare at heart and wants you to succeed."

I could never understand the logic of these words. If she really cared for me why would she always be telling tales about me?

In those days my daily routine began before ten in the morning when I left Dauji's house and went to my own home. After having breakfast there, I would proceed to school. My lunch would be sent to the school. After classes I would go home, fill up my lantern, and return to Dauji's. My dinner was despatched to his house.

When the courts were closed, Dauji would come and sit in the school compound and wait for me. On our way back he would shower me with questions about the day's schoolwork and expect me to give him a detailed account. Leaving me at my house, he would go for his walk. He devoted about ten days every month to writing petitions at the local court. Each petition earned him a few rupees. All his spare time at court was spent reading.

Bebe's tailoring work was good and it brought in enough money. Having been the main breadwinner of the family for a number of years, she exerted great authority over Dauji.

One day, contrary to my routine, I visited Dauji at the court. The courts had closed for the day and Dauji was sitting on a bench under the thatch of a nearby tea-shop, drinking jaggery tea. I walked slowly towards him, picked up his mat and, putting my arms around his shoulder, I said, "Today *I* have come to take you. Let's go home."

Without looking at me he gulped down his tea, paid one anna for it, and silently accompanied me. Mischievously, I threatened to tell Bebe about his secret visit to the tea-shop. Hiding his embarrassment behind a smile, he said, "The man makes good tea and the jaggery in it makes one's fatigue vanish. Don't tell your Bebe. She is sure to make an excessively unnecessary fuss." He continued in an anxious, dejected tone, "That is her innate nature."

Hearing this, I felt very sorry for Dauji. I had always wanted to do so much for him and that day, by promising to keep silent about the incident, I thought I had done my bit.

When I mentioned this to my mother, she started sending fruits, milk and sugar to Dauji's. Though the poor man never got to taste any of these, I rose in Bebe's estimation and she started treating me better.

I remember one morning I took a tumbler full of milk to Dauji's and found Bebe was not at home. She had gone with her friends to bathe in Baba Sawan's pond. Seeing the milk, Dauji suggested, "Let's make tea today. I'll go get some jaggery from the shop. Put the water on the fire."

Bibi quickly lit the fire, I filled the vessel, and she quickly set it on the chulha. Both of us sat on the chauki, chatting. When Dauji came back with the jaggery, he said, "The two of you start your work. I shall make tea today."

So Bibi got busy with the sewing machine and I became involved in practising the intricacies of direct and indirect speech.

Dauji kept fanning the fire and, as was his habit, he loudly dictated to me. "Galileo said, The earth revolves around the sun. Galileo found out that the earth revolves around the sun. Don't make the mistake of stating that the sun revolves around the earth."

The water boiled and Dauji, brimming with pleasure and swaying with excitement, recited his newly composed poem. Sprinkling tea leaves into the boiling water, he once again cautioned me, "Golu, don't ever forget what Galileo said."

The vessel was still on the chulha and Dauji, like an overexcited child, was looking at the bubbling liquid and repeating, "Golu ... Galileo ..."

I was laughing as I continued to do my work while Bibi smiled and ran her machine. All three of us were drowned in ecstasy, almost as if all the happiness in the town had descended on our house. Suddenly the door opened and Bebe arrived on the scene. Hearing her footsteps, Dauji turned around and his face lost all colour. Steam was rising from the polished vessel. Small bubbles of tea could be seen on the surface. The old man, the conductor of this forbidden activity, had been caught. Bebe advanced towards the fire to get a better look and Dauji said in an apologetic tone, "It's only tea."

Giving Dauji a couple of blows on his back, she said, "You old man, have you no shame? May you be damned, may a bomb strike you. Is this the age for you to drink tea? You had no one to fear since I was not at home. Does it matter to you if I die today or tomorrow? In which evil hour were you born and which unlucky stroke of destiny united our lives? ... Why doesn't death claim you? But then, why should it?"

Repeating these words, she advanced like a she-wolf, stood on the chauki, and with a piece of cloth, picked up the vessel and flung it on the floor. Scalding hot tea fell on Dauji's ankles and feet. Muttering "May you alone prosper," he hurried away to the sitting room like a guilty child. Seeing his hasty flight, Bibi and I could not control our laughter which echoed through the house, and bounced back from the walls. I was spared but Bebe took hold of Bibi's hair and screamed, "My enemy, what is the nature of your relationship with the old man? Tell me or I will kill you. Why did you hand over the keys to him?"

Bibi burst into tears. I, too, quietly crept into the sitting room. Dauji, seated on his chair, was caressing his feet. I cannot say why, but seeing him like that brought on a laughing fit. I thrust my face into an almirah and laughed uncontrollably. Dauji gestured to me to come closer and said, "We should be thankful to be let off so lightly."

After a pause he continued, "I am the most despicable of dogs. I am like that man on whose head that unfortunate old woman of Mecca used to throw garbage."

When I looked at him in astonishment, he continued, "A curse be upon me, a mere mortal, for making such a fuss over a few drops of hot water scalding me. May the Prophet intercede on my behalf and obtain Allah's grace, and save me from the fires of hell. May Ibrahim give me courage and Ayyub give me fortitude."

I asked Dauji, "Whom do you refer to?"

My question had hurt him, but he replied in affectionate tones, "Jan-e-pidar, don't ask me. If I were to give you an answer, I would disappoint the spirit of my master, my teacher. He was my master, my father and also my teacher. In a sense, he is also your teacher."

Then he folded his arms across his chest and began to speak. This was one of the rare occasions when I heard Dauji use such glorious expressions of address for another and humble ones for

---

That unfortunate old woman: This refers to the old woman of Mecca who used to throw filth at Prophet Mohammed to express her resentment of his preaching.

himself. His narrative took very long as it was interspersed with countless Persian verses and prayers for the benediction of the departed soul.

When he finished his story, I asked Dauji why he was so impressed with his teacher whose memory made him fold his hands countless times, and why he always referred to himself as the humble servant of the man.

Dauji smiled, "A man who transforms a fool into the universally recognized Munshi Chintaram deserves to be called a prophet and a master. How else can I describe him?"

I slowly crept under my quilt and, tucking myself in, gazed at Dauji, whose head had sunk low and who was looking at his feet and pressing his calves. Smiling to himself, he said, "What I was and what he has made of me! ... What an overpowering voice he had! Turning his head towards me, he asked me, an idler, a chaupalzada, to come closer. Leaning on my lathi, I went and stood near him. Boys from the neighbourhood and from nearby villages were sitting in a semi-circle around him, memorizing their lessons. It was a congregation of boys, not one of whom dared to look up from his work ... When I went near him, he told me that he saw me everyday, grazing my goats. Leave your charges to graze and come here to read and write, he said to me. Without waiting for an answer, he asked me my name and, in a rough, uncouth voice, I said, Chintu ... He smiled, then with a short laugh, asked, What is your full name? Must be Chintaram. I nodded. His pupils were now looking at me from the corners of their eyes. I was wearing a khadi kurta and a langot instead of pajamas, and crude leather footwear. A red cloth was tied around my head. My goats ..."

Interrupting his monologue, I asked, "Did you graze goats, Dauji?"

"Oh yes," he answered with pride, "I was a gadaria, a goatherd, and my father owned a dozen goats."

I gazed at him in wonder and quickly asked another question to satisfy my curiosity, "And your goats grazed near the school?"

Dauji pulled his chair closer to the charpai and resting his feet on the edge, continued, "Jan-e-pidar, even cities did not have schools in those days and I'm talking about a village. Had anyone ever heard of M B High School seventy years ago? It was my master's passion for teaching that made people here send their sons to learn a few basic things from him. He belonged to an illustrious family that was well-versed in matters temporal and divine. His father, besides being the only hakim in the district, was also an outstanding preacher. One of his ancestors was the Maharaja of Kashmir's chief munshi. Through his house ran the river of learning. Persian, Arabic, algebra, logic and medicine were the menials in his home. I was not destined to meet my master's father but I got to hear of his intellectual prowess through the words of his son. He shared a close camaraderie with Shefta and Hakim Momin Khan Momin. My master received his education under the able guidance of Hakim Azurdah."

Fearing that Dauji would make a digression, I quickly interrupted, "Did you start taking lessons from him?"

Replying in the affirmative, Dauji went on, "His words were so engrossing, his glance so captivating, if he chose to, he could transform ordinary mortals into men of learning ... I threw aside my lathi and quickly sat down on the floor near him. He then asked me to sit on the mat with the others but I said that for eighteen years I had been sitting on the ground and now it did not matter where I sat. He smiled and, drawing out a primer of alphabets from a wooden chest, intoned, Alif, bey, pey, te ..."

Dauji was now lost in his past and kept repeating these first four letters of the alphabet. After a while, he raised his hand and said, "On one side lay the rehett and the fishpond, on the other were the farmers' houses. My master's orchard and an old, imposing haveli lay between these two landmarks. It was in the orchard that he conducted his classes. His doors were always open to believers of all faiths and creeds."

After reflecting on his words for a long time, I framed another question with great caution, "What was the goodly name of your teacher?"

First he corrected my question and then replied, "Hazrat Ismael Ali Chishti, may Allah's grace be upon him! His father always called him Jan-e-jana but would occasionally address him as Mazhar Jan-e-jana."

I yearned to know more but Dauji stopped in the middle of his narrative and asked, "What is the Subsidiary System?"

May the English perish, whether they came in the guise of the East India Company or with a farman from Queen Victoria! They always presented obstacles in my path, always threw a spanner in the works. Like the arithmetic tables that I repeated mechanically, I droned whatever I knew about the Subsidiary System. Dauji then picked up the grammar book from the table and said, "Go and see if your Bebe's anger has now subsided."

Pretending to fill water in a dry ink bottle, I went outside and saw Bebe busy with her sewing machine and Bibi in the kitchen, cleaning up.

Bebe was an unpleasant factor in Dauji's life. Sometimes, when the usual scowl was absent from her face and the atmosphere in the house was conducive, Dauji would say, "Everyone will now recite a couplet."

Usually I was the first one asked and I would rapidly recite this particular one by Ghalib:

> *Why did you go away, leaving me alone?*
> *You should have waited for me*
> *Now that you have chosen to go,*
> *live on alone*

Dauji would clap his hands and say, "I refuse to listen to this oft-repeated couplet. I don't want to hear a narrative poem either and would prefer to hear less of Urdu."

I would ask for time to think and would suggest that Bibi recite something in the meantime. Like me, Bibi also had a Persian couplet which she would recite very often. Dauji would now say, "Order, order," and Bibi, putting down her scissors, would recite another. After praising her performance, Dauji would remind her that she had recited these lines quite often in the past. Then he would look at Bebe and say, "Now your Bebe will recite something."

Her standard, indifferent reaction used to be, "I don't know any couplets or poetry."

Dauji would then request her to at least sing some marriage songs, especially those celebrating the bridegroom's ride on a mare to the bride's house. Bebe would try to smile when he said this, but she could never really do it. Instead, Dauji would start singing like the women at weddings and, very often, Amichand's or my name would figure in the place of the groom's. Dauji would imagine the future and say, "When Golu gets married, I shall put on a red turban. Doctor Sahab and I will walk together in the baraat and I shall be one of the witnesses signing the marriage certificate."

Hearing these words, I would look down in embarrassment and he would say, "Somewhere in this land, in some little town, dwells my future daughter-in-law, a little girl, studying perhaps in class five or six. Once a week she will have her domestic science class and she will learn how to cook quite a few dishes. I am quite sure she is an intelligent student. This ignorant woman here cannot even classify animals according to gender but my daughter-in-law will be able to tell. I shall first teach the child Persian and then calligraphy. Then we will go on to writing in a slanted hand, which is unknown to most women. Golu, I shall live with you then. She and I will converse in Persian and you will look at us like a dunce."

Folding his hands across his chest, he would continue, "Jan-e-pidar, you work so hard. Shabash, well done!"

Sitting on his mat, poor Dauji would be lost in a world of dreams where he would be issuing orders in Persian. Once, when he was sitting on the terrace enjoying the sun, he said to me slowly, "May Allah grant Amichand a wife just like yours – obedient and respectable. I am not very happy with his ideology. All this – Sewa Sangh, the Muslim League and the Belcha Party – don't appeal to my way of thinking. Nor do I appreciate his learning martial arts or lathi-wielding and gathka-swinging. I don't know when the boy will listen to me. I only hope Allah gives him a gentle, respectable wife. Then he will be on the right path."

I was pained to hear these high expectations he had of his son and I became silent, knowing that if I said anything, I would hurt Dauji greatly. Though we often talked about my marriage and Amichand's, Bibi's wedding day actually arrived on the twelfth of

January. The groom, Ram Pratap, was held in great esteem by
Dauji because, he said, the boy had all the qualities Dauji had
greatly desired and wished for. Perhaps Dauji's greatest source of
happiness lay in the knowledge that the groom's father was a teacher
of Persian and had affiliations with the Kabirpanthi sect. When the
time came for Bibi to depart with her husband, a pall of gloom
descended over the house. A steady stream of tears poured down
Bebe's face; Amichand also wept and the womenfolk from the
neighbourhood joined them. I stood near a wall beside Dauji.
Putting his arm around my shoulders, Dauji repeatedly said, "I
seem to be floating in air today and appear to have lost my balance."

The groom's father then asked Dauji for permission to leave
and, hearing him, Bibi fainted. She was put on a charpai and the
women fanned her. Leaning on me, Dauji walked towards the
recumbent Bibi and lifted her up. "What is this, Beta? Sit up. This
is the beginning of a new and independent life for you. Don't
make it an inauspicious moment by crying."

Bibi clung to Dauji, weeping loudly. Running his hand over her
head, he continued, "Qurratulain, I am a sinner for not having
educated you, and for not bestowing on you the treasure of
knowledge. You and Ram Pratap might excuse me but I shall
never be able to forgive myself for this lapse. I am, indeed, a
sinner and my head hangs in shame before you."

Bibi cried louder on hearing this and tears coursed down Dauji's
face. Ram Pratap's father stepped forward and reassured Dauji,
"Munshiji, don't worry. I shall teach her the Karimah."

Dauji, with folded hands, said, "She has read the Karimah and
has also gone through *Gulistan* and *Bostaan* but my yearning to
teach her more remains."

"That is the limit," replied the groom's father. "Even I have not fully read these works. I even skipped over the Arabic terms whenever I came across them in the text."

Dauji stood with folded hands for a long time. Bibi drew her hand out from under her silken shawl and ran it first over Amichand's head and then over mine. She was escorted by her friends towards the door. Dauji, leaning on me, also walked along and suddenly, embracing me tightly, he said, "Look, you are also weeping. You, who are my support. Tears falling from a man's eyes? What has happened to you? Jan-e-pidar, why ..."

His voice choked and my tears flowed faster. By now the groom's party had climbed into their tongas and ekkas. Bibi was seated in a rath and Dauji, Amichand and I walked behind it. If Bibi's wailing became too loud, Dauji would hasten forward and, drawing aside the curtain at the window, say, "Stop weeping, Beta, at this auspicious hour."

The end of his turban was wet with tears.

Rano was notorious in our mohalla. His whole being was imbued with evil and he had a specially malicious nature. The cattle-shed which I have mentioned earlier, had about twenty, twenty-five goats and a couple of cows. Every morning and evening he would sell their milk in the adjoining field. Practically everyone in the mohalla bought milk from this man, whose notoriety made them fear him. Whenever he passed our house he would bang his lathi on the ground and call out, mockingly, to Dauji, "Panditan, jai Ramji ki."

Dauji would then clarify that he did not belong to the pandit community which was a highly learned one.

Rano would ignore what he said and, biting his lips, retort,

"Those who grow bodhis on the back of their heads are all pandits."

Rano was always in the company of rogues and scoundrels, and, in the evenings, the cattle-shed became a gambling den or a venue for sessions of obscene poetry. One day, after Bibi's wedding, when I went to get milk from him, he gave me a sidelong glance and asked tauntingly, "The bewitching morni has gone now. Why are you staying on?"

Observing my silence, he stirred the frothy milk with the ladle and said, "Tell me truthfully, did you take a dip in the Ganga flowing in the house or not?"

I struck him on the head with the milk pail. Though no blood flowed, Rano staggered and fell on to the charpai nearby and I rushed home. After I told Dauji about this, I ran home and told my father what had happened. Rano was summoned to the police station where the havaldar, after admonishing him and delivering a few light strokes with the baton, sent him home.

Since that day Rano took to passing lewd comments on Dauji and took perverse pleasure in making fun of Bebe. He would do this each time he saw Dauji. There was no doubt that Dauji's bodhi looked ridiculous. But he had an explanation for keeping it. "This is a memento of my late mother and is as precious to me as my life. She would place my head in her lap and, after washing it with curd, massage it with mustard oil till it shone. Though I never dared to take off my turban in front of my revered teacher, he knew about my little bodhi. Once, when I came home for vacations, after I started working at the Dayalchand Memorial High School, he asked me, I hope you have not shorn off your hair in the city? I immediately replied in the negative. He was happy to hear my answer and said that few women could boast of such obedient sons. He said that he was indeed lucky to have the honour of teaching a student like me. Touching his feet, I said, Huzoor, don't embarrass me. I consider it a blessing to try and follow in your footsteps. No, no, he said, And don't touch my feet, Chintaram. What is the use of doing something which I cannot even feel? Tears welled up in my eyes and I said that I would part oceans to find a cure for his legs. I would give up my life in exchange for this cure, but I was helpless. After a pause, he said, If Allah has willed it, I accept my fate ... May you live long for carrying me around the village on your back, these past ten years!"

Dauji, by now, was totally immersed in his past. He continued, "Early in the morning I would enter the doorway of his house and say, Your humble servant is here. The ladies of the house would move away and my teacher would call me in. Considering myself fortunate to be summoned, I would walk towards him with folded hands, touch his feet and wait for instructions. He would bless me, ask after my parents, the news in the village and then say, Now, Chintaram, you can pick up this bundle of sins. I would lift him up tenderly, almost as if I was handling a delicate blossom, and carry him outside the house. Sometimes he would ask to be taken to the orchard, sometimes to the rehett. Once in a while, he would request me, very gently, If it is not too tiring, take me to the mosque today. In spite of my willingness to take him there everyday, he never accepted my offer. He said that he did not wish to go there everyday and whenever he did, he would tell me. On these occasions I would take him to the chabootara where ablutions were performed before prayers, take off his soft shoes, put them in a bag, and sit leaning against the wall of the mosque. From the chabootara he would drag himself to a place in the line of men standing for namaaz. I saw this only once. I never had the courage to watch it again and I always hid my face in the folds of my garments, looking up only when I heard him call my name. On the way back, I carried him through the long, meandering streets of the town before taking him home. He would say, Chintaram, I know you take me around to please me but I am greatly pained. Firstly, you have to bear my weight as I am carried about. Secondly, I feel guilty for wasting so much of your time. How could I e.:plain to him that these were the most elevating moments in my life and my discomfort was the centre of my being? He would say, I am fit only to be carried about. Little did he know that to me he was Huma, the legendary bird that brought good luck to those on whom it alighted. The day I learnt and recited the *Sikandarnama* for him, he was ecstatic, as if he had become the monarch of the seven skies. He showered countless blessings on me and, running his affectionate hands over my head, gave me a rupee which he extracted from his pocket, as a reward. I kissed this coin which was, to me, more sacred than the black stone of the Kaaba. Holding it reverently in my hands, pretending to be one of Sikandar's officers, I tucked it into the folds of my turban. With both hands raised, he continued to bless me, You have done what I could never achieve. You are a good man on whom Allah has bestowed His kindness. Chintaram, you are a descendant of Moosa, a herdsman like you by profession and a follower of prophets, on whom Allah bestows His boundless grace. Allah showers His benediction on you and will do so ever more ..." Suddenly Dauji put his hands on his knees and fell silent.

My examinations were about to begin and Dauji was becoming a hard taskmaster. He gave me assignments to keep me busy at all times. The moment I finished one topic, he asked me to study another. If I went to drink water, he would follow me like a shadow and bombard me with questions about dates in history. He made it a habit to reach school in the evenings. I escaped from him one day by creeping out through the boarding house gates instead of stepping out through the main entrance. He took to sitting outside the classroom after this episode.

I had become irritable and rude, and my oft-repeated phrase was, "You wretch of a Dauji." When he or his questions became tough, I did not hesitate to call him a cur. This would anger him and he would say, "Look at yourself, you Domni, what language you use? When your wife comes, I shall tell her how abusive you were and that you often called me a cur." If he was very angry he would call me an incorrigible domni. No matter how angry he was, he never said anything harsher than this. He hardly ever addressed me by my real name. When referring to my elder brother, he would either say, Aftab Beta or Master Aftab but for me he used to coin new names everyday. Though Golu was his favourite, he sometimes called me the noisy tamboora.

Once, he gave me a problem in algebra to solve, and sat on the charpai, reading. I was overcome with impatience. Deciding to irritate him, I kicked my books aside and started clapping and singing a loud and ridiculous song. His eyes glinted with laughter as he peered over his spectacles, came over to me, opened my notebook at the page where I was supposed to be writing, and then placed his big hand between my clapping palms.

"That's enough, Beta," he said, "It isn't such a difficult problem."

As soon as he lowered his head to explain, I started to clap again. He then asked in expectant tones, "Am I not your Dauji?"

"No," I said loudly.

"Then who am I?" he asked sadly.

Pointing at the sky, I remarked, "That is the true Sarkar. He sustains us all ... Now you tell me who reigns over the earth?"

He made a move to go away but I quickly put my hands around his waist and asked, "Angry with me, Dauji?"

Smiling, he replied, "Let me go, my tamboora ... Leave me, Beta. I was only going to get a drink of water."

In mock irritation I replied, "Just see, when it comes to solving my problem, Dauji remembers he is thirsty."

He sat down and, opening my notebook, said, "Why did you not apply the fourth formula when you had to find out the root of one-fourth? Even if you had forgotten to do this then ..."

By now Dauji had forgotten all about his thirst.

Another incident took place in the second week of February. There was just a month and a half left for the examinations and I was assailed by a sense of great fear about the future. Of my own volition, I had stepped up the pace of work and tried to become a serious student. Despite Dauji's best efforts, I could never solve geometrical problems. He suggested that the only way out was to learn the fifty two theorems in geometry by heart. I got busy doing that. My only problem was that by morning I had forgotten all that I had learnt at night. I lost heart. My courage seemed to have deserted me.

One night Dauji also looked quite tense after making me practise geometrical constructions and related exercises. As I stumbled through them, Dauji's tension was visible. He asked me to go to sleep and went away to his room. When he had gone, I took up my book once again and, till well past midnight, attempted to learn things by heart. Each time I closed my book to write what I had learnt, I realized that I could remember nothing beyond the first few phrases. The memory of Dauji's disappointed face and the awareness of my own incompetence brought tears to my eyes and I went out and sat on the steps of the verandah. After a while I started weeping. I put my head on my knees and shivered in the cold. I must have sat like this for almost two hours when it occurred to me that the only way I could save Dauji's honour was by walking out of the front door and never returning. Having made up my mind, I raised my head and saw Dauji standing next to me, draped in a blanket. He drew me close to him and the courtyard was filled with the sound of sobbing. Kissing my forehead, Dauji said, "Look here, tamboora, I never knew you were such a coward."

Then, wrapping me in his blanket, he took me to the sitting room, made me sit on the bed, tucked the blanket around me and sat down in a chair. He told me that, though geometry was a difficult subject, I should not allow it to scare me. It had in the past created difficulties for him also. He had gone through all the books of geometrical theory and practice at his teacher's house and had taken copious notes. There seemed to be no aspect of the subject that he had not grasped. "I thought I had achieved excellence in mathematical derivations," said Dauji, "but one night, as I was lying in bed grappling with an issue related to parallelograms, I got deeply entangled in a problem. I lit my lamp and, making a face, pondered over the problem. I arrived at the right answer through algebraic procedures but could not do the same through geometrical ones. All night I filled up sheets of paper with calculations, but I did not cry like you in the face of defeat. Early next morning, I presented myself before my teacher, who with his blessed hands started solving the problem. Like me, he also got stuck at the same point and said, Chintaram, I can teach you no more, and when the teacher and the taught reach the same plane of knowledge, it is time for the latter to seek another source of learning. Hearing this, I said, Had I heard another saying these words I would consider them to be sacrilegious. Since they come from you, I consider each word to be a commandment of Allah's. Could I ever dare to differ from you, my master? Yet, I am deeply hurt. He replied, You are a very sensitive man. You should at least appreciate what I have said to you. Bowing my head, I sought his advice, which he readily gave. In Delhi, he told me, lives Hakim Nasir Ali Seestani, a man of great proficiency in the science of numbers. If you are so interested in it you could go to him and draw upon his knowledge. I shall write him a note. As I indicated my inclination to go, he told me to consult my mother first and then get back to him after obtaining her consent. I knew it was impossible to get my mother's permission so I never sought it. When my teacher asked if I had done as he had asked, I lied to him, saying that our house was being whitewashed and once the job was done, I would speak to her. Days passed in a state of restlessness as I tried to think of a way out. I craved to go to Delhi but I could not leave without permission and his letter of introduction. His permission would not be forthcoming till I had my mother's permission and, in her old age, I knew she would never agree. One night, when the whole village slept and I was just as perturbed as you are now, I opened my mother's basket and from her savings I stole two rupees. I made my way out of the village. May Allah forgive me and may the spirits of my ancestors always be kind to me! I had committed a grievous sin and, on till Eternity, my head would hang in shame before these generous souls. Leaving the village behind, I walked towards my revered teacher's haveli and reached the place behind it which served as a classroom. I knelt and kissed the ground, saying to myself, I am an unfortunate creature to be leaving without your permission and I shall eternally crave your blessings. If you don't forgive me, I shall lay my life down at your feet. Then I picked up my lathi, placed it on my shoulder and walked away ... Are you listening?" Dauji asked after giving me a close look.

"Yes," I replied feebly from the depths of my quilt and blinked.

Dauji continued, "Destiny gave me a helping hand. In those days, the railroad connecting Jakhal, Jind, Sirsa and Hissar was being laid. This railroad went on ahead to Delhi and I was lucky to get some work on this project. I'd work for one day and then walk for the next two. With the help of some unseen power I reached Delhi after sixteen days. I had arrived at my destination but had still to achieve my objective. Whenever I asked about the residence of Hakim Nasir Ali Seestani, I met with disappointment. For two days I tried to locate his house but was unsuccessful. But luck was on my side and my health was good. I again managed to get work on a site where bungalows were being constructed for the British. In the evenings, when I was free, I would try to find out Hakim Sahab's address. When night came, I sought the shelter of a dharamshala, where I slept soundly on my mat. As they say, Jo inda woh binda. I tried hard and finally I succeeded. I got to know where he lived. His house was situated in a gali in the stone-breakers mohalla. I presented myself before him one evening. He lived in a small room and when I saw him for the first time, he was involved in an animated conversation with his friends. Taking off my shoes, I stepped over the threshold and stood still. One gentleman enquired, Who are you? I said that I had come to see Hakim Sahab. In the centre of the circle sat Hakimji and his back was towards me. Without turning around, he asked, Who are you? I replied, I have come from Punjab and ... Even before I had finished, he said loudly, Are you Chintaram? I was at a loss for words but he went on to say, I have received a letter from Usman Ali. He speaks of Chintaram's arrival and mentions that the lad has run away from home without informing anyone. He has asked me to extend some assistance ... I stood silent for a while and even when I stepped forward, he did not turn his head. Then he spoke in a commanding manner, Barkhurdar, sit down. He requested his friends to wait as he wanted to get to know me. Which numerical derivation have you been unable to solve? he asked. I stated the problem and saw him place his hands on his shoulders and pull up his kurta so high that his waist was exposed. With your finger, he told me, draw the geometrical figure on my back. I was stunned. I had neither the strength to go forward nor could I draw back. After a moment's pause, he continued, Hurry up, lad. I'm a blind man who knows nothing about pen and paper. Fearfully I stepped forward and on his smooth, broad back I drew the particular diagram with shaking fingers. When I finished, he asked me to connect all the points in the figure. On the one hand I was tense, on the other I could not see anything on his back. I quickly placed my finger wherever I could and started to draw. He corrected me, Where are you drawing? That is not the correct point ... You'll get used to my method with time. Place your finger about six inches below my shoulder and start drawing from there. I praise Allah for Hakim Sahab's vast knowledge, his sharp wit and his wonderful voice. When he spoke, I was dumbfounded. I always imagined that the figures I drew on his back would stand out in clear lines and be illuminated in bright light ..."

Dauji was now lost in the memories of Delhi. Though his eyes were wide open and he seemed to be looking at me, his attention was obviously elsewhere. I asked him impatiently, "What happened then?"

Rising from his chair, he replied, "It's very late now. I'll tell you another time."

Like a stubborn child I insisted. So Dauji said, "Promise me first that you will not be disheartened and that insignificant geometry propositions will not appear insurmountable ... To put it briefly, I remained at Hakim Sahab's place for almost a year but drew just a few drops from his vast ocean of knowledge. On my return home I went straight to my teacher and placed my head at his feet. He said, Chintaram, if it were in my power I would draw back my feet. I wept at his words and, with loving hands, he touched my head and said, I am not angry with you but a year's absence is an unbearably long time. If you ever go away again take me with you." Dauji's eyes swam with tears as he narrated this and he walked out of the room, leaving me lost in my thoughts.

With the examinations round the corner my blood seemed to freeze but I was getting bulkier. This worried Dauji. He would often hold my hand and say, "Try to be a horse, not a donkey."

I resented these words and, as a mark of protest, I would stop speaking to him. My silence did not move him and I saw his concern growing into anxiety. One morning, before he went out for his constitutional, despite my pleas, protests, abuses and wails, he made me stand up and put on my coat. Then, grabbing my shoulders, he dragged me out. It was about four o'clock on a dark, cold winter morning and there was not a soul on the street. I was being extremely uncivil and he said, "You have not yet overcome your sleep, tamboora, and so you are grumbling ... Speak up ... Say something."

When we had left our town far behind and the chilly morning air had forced open my eyes, Dauji let go of my shoulder. We passed by the rehett of the sardars, walked past the river and the graveyard, but Dauji strode on, mumbling some Quranic verses. I was petrified when we reached a particular hillock. People avoided walking here even in the afternoons as it was believed that a city had mysteriously sunk and vanished from this site in days gone by. The restless spirits of the dead were said to roam here and devour those who came near. As I trembled with fear, Dauji adjusted my muffler and said, "Can you see the two keekar trees in the distance? Walk briskly between them ten times, draw many deep breaths and then come to me. I am sitting here."

To save myself from that horrible place, I walked quickly towards the trees he had indicated. First, I sat to rest on a boulder and estimated how much time one would take to complete six rounds. Imagining that the requisite time for this was over, I made myself visible to him and ran four rounds. Then I sat down on a boulder and inhaled deeply. Strange sounds of birds could be heard emanating from the trees, when a sharp pain seared my rib cage. I thought it was now appropriate to go and wake Dauji who seemed to be dozing. I wanted to take him home and make myself

comfortable. Filled with anger and shivering with terror, I reached the place where Dauji had been sitting. He had now fallen on his knees and, like a demented soul, was reciting his favourite verse:

Don't betray in love,
Lest, on Judgement Day, you stand shamed
Before lovers ...

Sometimes he would interrupt this recital by hitting the ground with his palms, looking up, raising his index finger as if he could see someone standing before him, and say threateningly, "Think awhile. I'm telling you, I'm informing you ..." Writhing, he fell on the gravel but kept repeating the same verses and sobbed.

For a while I stood absolutely still, watching him. Then I gave a loud scream and, in panic, ran towards the keekar trees instead of heading towards the town. Dauji seemed to know the magical incantations that brought djinns under human control and he started uttering them there. With my own eyes I saw a djinn standing before him. It looked like a being out of *The Arabian Nights*. Dauji's incantations obviously failed to enslave it. He was thrown to the ground but he kept repeating his chant. Dauji then started to scream but the djinn held him in his clutches. I sat on a boulder and wept. After a while, Dauji came to me and, with his usual expression, said, "Let's go home, tamboora."

I hastened after him. He took the four corners of his unwound turban in his hands and, all the way back, he swayed and sang songs.

As I was walking behind him, I saw Dauji's being undergo a transformation. Long locks of matted hair seemed to hang from his head and cover his whole body. Even if someone had threatened me with dire consequences, I could never have dared to go for another walk with Dauji.

A few days after this incident a shower of broken bricks and clods of earth rained down upon our house. Bebe was infuriated with Dauji and became as hostile as a bitch with pups. She attacked him, threw him to the ground and shouted, "You old totki, this is all your doing. It's your kaala ilm, your black magic that has descended upon us. Your demons pelt the house with stones, wanting death and desolation."

Then she took to screaming loudly, "I am dead. I've been destroyed. This man is now making plans to take Amichand's life. He has cast a spell over me and all my limbs are broken."

How could Dauji become inimical towards Amichand whom he treasured more than his life? Yet Dauji was responsible for stones being thrown at the house. When I agreed with Bebe, Dauji, for the first time, reprimanded me and called me a fool and Bebe, a child of illiteracy. "The result of a year's teaching," he said ironically, "has resulted in you believing in djinns and demons. I am greatly disappointed. It is a pity that you have chosen to be swayed by the sentimentality of a woman rather than relying upon rationality."

Leaving Dauji sighing and Bebe shouting, I went up and sat on the terrace.

That evening, as I was returning home, I encountered Rano on the way. He asked, with a knowing look, "Tell me, did any of the stones hit you? I hear that stones rained upon your master's house."

Without replying I entered the passageway. At night, when Dauji was helping me with geometry, he happened to ask, "Do you believe in bhoots, djinns, paris and chudails, Beta?"

When I answered in the affirmative, he laughed and said, "You really are innocent. I should not have reprimanded you today. Why didn't you tell me earlier that djinns actually exist and are capable of pelting stones? I needlessly called masons to construct the portico when I could easily have summoned the assistance of djinns. Tell me, can they lay bricks or are they only capable of pelting stones?"

"You can afford to laugh now, Dauji, but the day you crack your skull, you will change your mind," I snapped.

He then said, "Your djinn cannot do this till Qayamat because it does not exist and, therefore, it cannot lift bricks and pelt them at you or me or your Bebe ... There is a basic principle of physics which states that physical matter cannot be moved by the non-physical. Do you understand?"

"I do."

Though there was a school in our town, the matric examinations were not held here. We had to go to the district headquarters for this purpose. The day came when my classmates and I got into a lorry and went for the examinations. Around the lorry stood a group of people, probably parents, so how could Dauji be anywhere else? While everyone's parents prayed for the success of their wards, he shot questions at me and then answered them himself. From the reforms of Akbar to climatic changes, we covered a vast number of topics. He would suddenly ask me to identify the king who looked like a Hindu, remained usually intoxicated, and was always with a woman.

"Jahangir," I replied quickly.

"And the woman?"

"Noorjehan," we answered in unison.

Then came questions on grammar which I was asked to answer with examples. To escape Dauji's clutches, I entered the lorry after the others had boarded it. He, however, made his way to where I was sitting and continued pestering me with questions.

"Use Break in and Break into in sentences of your own," he demanded. I did so. When the lorry started moving his last words were about gender. It was thus after a year that I got rid of Dauji and tasted freedom.

I fared quite well in the history examination on the first day. I did even better in the geography one on the second day. The third day was a Sunday and the following day was the mathematics examination. On Sunday morning I received a page-long letter from Dauji. All of it was devoted to algebraic formulae and mathematical derivations.

I compared notes with other boys after the examination and found that I had correctly attempted questions worth eighty marks. I was so overjoyed that I felt I was walking on air and my heart was singing. Just as I stepped out from the verandah, I saw Dauji looking at another boy's question paper. Giving a shout of joy, I embraced him and chanted, "Eighty marks ... I should get eighty marks."

He snatched my paper from my hands and asked with bitterness, "Where did you go wrong?"

I swayed and said, "The one that had to do with four walls."

He was furious, "I am sure you forgot to deduct the area of the doors and windows."

Holding him by the waist, I said, "Oh, let's now forget about the doors and windows."

In a sinking voice, he replied, "The whole year's effort has been

wasted. If you remember, tamboora, I was constantly reminding you to be very careful while doing derivations concerning area. You never listened to me ... You never did. Now you've lost twenty marks, full twenty marks."

Dauji's fallen face made me feel that my achievement worth eighty marks was less than the loss of twenty. On the way back he kept telling himself that if the examiner was generous, he would surely give me one mark for that section which was correct. After this paper, Dauji stayed on till the last day of the examination and each day he would tutor me till midnight and then he would go and spend the night at a friend's house. He would be back in the morning at eight and accompany me to the examination centre.

Once the examination was over I made a clean break from Dauji. The whole day I would roam around with my friends and in the evenings, I would read novels. Occasionally, if I had the time, I would go to pay my respects to him. He would insist that I spend an hour with him everyday so that he could prepare me for higher studies. I did not fall into his trap. I would rather fail in college a hundred times than be his student again. It had become so difficult to even converse with him. Each time I asked him a question he would either ask me to translate it into Persian or analyze it grammatically. When the hawaldar's cow entered the house and I tried to drive it away, he asked me, "Is Cow a noun or a verb?"

Anyone who has studied till class five can say that it is a noun but he stated, "It could be both a noun and a verb. To cow means to threaten."

All this happened during the days following the examination. A day came when some of us planned to go hunting and I warned my friends that we should not go by the courts as we were sure to run into Dauji. He would definitely stop us to question me about proverbs that concerned guns and cartridges. If I ever happened to see him in the market, I would quickly enter a bylane. Whenever I visited him, I would now spend more time talking with Bebe than with him. Sometimes, he would say, "It's a pity that you, too, have forsaken me like Aftab."

I would only laugh.

The day my results were announced, my father bought some laddoos and we went to his house. We found Dauji sitting with his head bowed but when he saw his visitor, he got up to get a chair. Placing it near his mat, he said, "Doctor Sahab, I feel embarrassed facing you but then, such are the ways of destiny. I had thought that he would secure a first division but it was not to be. He lacked a strong foundation."

"I missed it just by one mark," I interrupted cheerfully.

Dauji looked at me and said, "I am heartbroken about that one mark. But such is Allah's will."

While Dauji and my father talked, I became engrossed in conversation with Bebe.

I soon joined college and, in the beginning, I was prompt in answering Dauji's letters. Gradually, our correspondence grew irregular and then dwindled away all together. When I came home for the vacations I would pay my respects to Dauji as I would to other teachers. Now he did not throw any questions at me and was happy to see me dressed in coats, pants and ties. He would not allow me to sit on a charpai any more and would say, "If you won't allow me to pull a chair for you then you can pull one for yourself." I would do as he suggested and sit near him. He would always express a desire to see the books that I may have brought from the college library and made it a point to come to my house to read them.

Amichand had left college for some reason and joined a bank in Delhi. Bebe continued to sew the neighbours' clothes as usual and Dauji continued to go to the courts though he did not earn anything. Bibi's letters spoke of marital bliss in her new home. A year at college drew me away from Dauji even more.

Vacations during the second year of college were spent on trivialities. A long journey to Abbotabad was very interesting. During my visit there, I bought, for the first time in my life, a pink coloured writing pad and envelopes, knowing fully well that I could not write either to my father or to Dauji on this kind of stationery. The Dusshera and Christmas holidays went by and I did not meet Dauji. A considerable time passed by like this.

The nation gained its independence and riots broke out. Gradually, the tempo of violence increased and one frequently heard of turbulent incidents. Though our town was free from such occurrences, traders shut down their businesses and fled. The people of the town overlooked this phenomenon but, after a few days, refugees started trickling in. They brought the news that we had indeed got independence.

Just a few days later, some houses were set on fire and skirmishes broke out in two localities. The police, along with the military, imposed curfew in the town. When it was lifted, the Hindus and Sikhs left the place.

One afternoon my mother sent me to enquire about Dauji.

When I entered the familiar mohalla I saw a number of strange, unknown faces on the street. On entering Dauji's house, I saw a bullock tethered in the passageway. A dirty, coarse curtain was hanging behind the animal. I came back home and told my mother that Dauji and Bebe had abandoned their home and would never return. I could not believe that he had betrayed us like this.

Three days later I was returning home in the evening from the mosque. I had gone there to note down the names of the refugees and had promised to send them blankets.

On my way back, I happened to pass through Dauji's gali and I saw more than a hundred people in the open field nearby. Refugee children, with lathis in their hands, could be heard shouting abuses. I tried to push my way through the crowd to get to the middle. The hostile looks of the refugees dissuaded me from doing so. I then heard a young man telling an elderly gentleman, "He had gone to a nearby village and, on his return, he walked straight into his house."

"Which house?" the old man asked.

"The house of the refugees from Rohtak," came the answer.

"Then?" asked the elder.

"Then what?" said the man, "They caught hold of him and he turned out to be a Hindu."

Then someone from the crowd shouted loudly, "Come quickly, Rano ... Hurry up, here's your man ... the pandit ..."

Rano, who was driving his goats towards their pen, caught hold of a boy with a lathi and asked him to mind the animals. He then pushed his way into the crowd.

My heart stopped beating for a moment as I knew that it was Dauji who had been cornered. Without having actually seen the

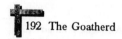

victim, I told the people nearby, "He is a good man ... He is a noble soul. Don't accuse him of anything. He is ..."

A number of bloodshot eyes looked at me and a young man, with a cleaver in his hands, said, "Shall I teach you a lesson also? Coming here to sympathize! You cannot imagine what has happened to others."

In fright I pushed myself into another section of the crowd. I saw that at Rano's instigation, his friends had surrounded Dauji. Rano himself had taken hold of the man's chin and was saying, "First cut off his bodhi ... His lock of hair ..."

Then, with a serrated sickle, he did what he was saying. The young man asked, "Shall we make him say his last prayers?"

Rano replied, "Forget it, he's an old man. He can graze goats with me."

Once again he took hold of Dauji's chin and said, "Recite the Kalma, pandit."

"Which one?" asked Dauji softly.

Rano gave him a hard slap across his head and Dauji almost fell.

"Saale," he spat out, "are there four or five Kalmas?"

When Dauji finished, Rano handed him his lathi and said, "Go. The goats are waiting for you."

Unturbanned, Dauji started walking behind the goats, like a long-haired Baba Farid.

Baba Farid: A sufi mystic of Punjab.

A Palace in Paradise

Sajid Rashid

translated by Naghma Zafir

As was his habit, Mushtaque got ready for his morning namaaz. He bowed in a ruku and a sharp belch rose in his throat. His mouth was filled with the bitter taste of liquor consumed the night before and of acidic digestive juices. When he prostrated in the sijda, the red satin ribbon around those voluptuous hips danced before his eyes, its knotted ends swaying like a snake with every twist and thrust of the slender waist. Tiny drops of perspiration winked and flashed like thousands of neon bulbs round the depths of that navel, and instead of chanting Subhana-rabiul Ala, Praise be to the Lord God, the Almighty, he inadvertently uttered, Subahan Allah!

Subahan Allah! Praise be to god! Startled by his slip, he checked himself, and hurriedly said his Salaam. He recited the Lahaul to rid himself of the devil, and then folded up his prayer mat.

Last night he had had a drink too many and the different types of liquor with their varied effects had managed to upset his stomach. The present series of sour belches were the outcome of the havoc those drinks had played with his digestive system. Usually he turned down his glass after three pegs. But last night the Egyptian belly dancer Jakiya's swaying hips and the fast-paced music seemed to have fired his thirst.

After his namaaz, he quickly shaved and bathed and, as usual, had just a cup of tea. Then, reciting the Darud-sharif, a homage to the holy Prophet and all his holy kin, he left for office.

Caught in the throng of the first class compartment of the local train, he thought of the party the previous night and burned with embarrassment. The party had been organized by his office. He had succeeded in securing an important and lucrative tender for a Sudanese company. It was the first important foreign tender that this company had got through him so the General Manager decided to throw a party for the office executives at The Oberoi to celebrate his success. There, in an attempt to capture the moon of the Egyptian belly dancer's navel in his goblet, Mushtaque had drowned himself in it instead.

It was not the number of drinks he had had that he regretted as much as the fact that he had missed his morning prayer. Ever since his school days the fajr prayer had been a part of his daily routine. He had been brought up on the strict "No namaaz, no breakfast!" principle. So if he missed his fajr prayer then he felt uneasy throughout the day, as though something was amiss.

As soon as he reached the office he was reminded by the Project Manager that the evening's hospitality for the Sudanese guest had to include not only a chilled bottle of bubbly champagne but a Filipino girl too. These days people from Africa and the Middle East showed great interest in Filipino girls. Earlier, they used to be crazy about fair-complexioned ones. He had once asked the Project Manager why they were so keen on these short-statured Filipinos now. The Manager had winked meaningfully and said, "To each his own."

Mushtaque assured the Project Manager that he would do everything possible to satisfy their guest, and then called up Quadir. For a long time the phone kept ringing. Mushtaque's heart beat faster, warning him that if he failed to make the necessary arrangements and the Sudanese guest was disappointed, he would be held responsible for the fiasco. Suddenly Benjamin's face swam before his eyes. Now, he had been an expert at handling such matters! But he had become an alcoholic and Mushtaque had been promoted to this position in his place. The moment the receiver was picked up at the other end, Benjamin's face vanished, the way a scene disappears when a fuse blows and the lights go off. Quadir's voice sounded gruff. Perhaps he had been sleeping. Quadir's job was such that when the city wound up its business for the day, his work began.

"Quadir, a Filipino girl is needed tonight."

"Where?"

"The Oberoi, Suite 432."

"Time?"

"From 10 till 11."

"Okay," Quadir said and hung up.

Mushtaque remembered the first time, six months ago, when he had been asked to entertain a client – an Arab sheikh. It had been raining heavily that day. As they drove down from Malabar Hill to Chowpatty, the sheikh had expressed a desire to say the evening maghrib prayers. But they couldn't find a mosque on the way. Noting his keen interest in namaaz, the preconceived notion of immoral licentious sheikhs imprinted on Mushtaque's mind began to dissolve. He had, in fact, begun to feel ashamed of himself for thinking so badly of the man. But, vanishing with the rapidly moving wheels of the car, this feeling did not last even for a kilometre. For, the next moment, the sheikh had asked him, smiling, "Can you arrange for a good-looking teenage girl?"

Mushtaque felt as if the wild waves at Marine Drive were not dashing against the stone embankment but had instead delivered a resounding slap on his face. And, though the waves had sprayed the footpath with a million drops of foam, behind the closed windows of the car Mushtaque found his face drenched. He saw the sheikh staring intently at him as he waited for an answer. The sheikh's face, which had shone with piety a moment ago, seemed to Mushtaque to have acquired an evil glow.

"Are you listening? I need a teenage ..." said the sheikh, scratching his french beard, but to Mushtaque it seemed as if the man had put his hand inside his long aba and was scratching his thigh.

Mushtaque had a strong urge to either get out of the car or to push the sheikh out of it. Instead, he felt as if he was the one being thrown out. And, as he rolled down the road, the sheikh and Benjamin were watching him from the car with contempt in their eyes and raucous laughter on their lips.

After he had finished his MBA, Mushtaque had got this job with great difficulty and did not want to lose it by doing something that would jeopardize his reputation for efficiency. He took out his purse and, from among the many visiting cards that were stuffed in it, picked out Quadir's. The General Manager had given it to him, saying, "This man is very useful for our business. He can provide all that is needed to entertain a client." With trembling fingers he had dialled Quadir's number that day. And all the while he had felt as if he was committing the sin of touching a na-mehram, something forbidden to him.

The moment he mentioned the company's name Quadir had asked, "Where is Benjamin Saab?" Mushtaque briefly explained that Benjamin had been given another job and he had been assigned Benjamin's duties. From the familiar manner in which Quadir had enquired after Benjamin, it was evident that the two were old friends.

Just saying "Arrange for a girl" had made Mushtaque break into a cold sweat. He stammered as he gave the rest of the details. When he finished speaking, Quadir had guffawed, "Be frank, man! We are both in the same business." Quadir's loud laughter and the remark that followed grated on Mushtaque's ears. If only the man had been in front of him! He would have grabbed him by his shirt front and, shaking him hard, would have asked, "Where does the similarity lie, tell me? Is your business the same as mine, haan?"

At the specified hour Quadir had arrived at the hotel with a dusky girl of about eighteen or twenty. Quadir himself was about forty or forty-five. Against his stark white clothes, his swarthy complexion made a startling contrast. A lock of salt and pepper hair fell on his forehead. The girl looked embarrassed and impressed. The sheikh approved of her instantly and, as he looked at her, his face took on an even more sinister hue. Putting his arm around her waist, he thanked Mushtaque and Quadir. But Mushtaque felt he was actually dismissing him, saying, "Get out."

"Who will shell out the money?" Quadir had asked in a casually professional tone. That was when it suddenly struck Mushtaque that he had to pay for this from the company's entertainment fund. Quadir quoted a figure. Mushtaque hastily drew out the money from his wallet and handed it to Quadir. Quadir licked his thumb, counted the cash, then laughed, showing teeth stained with paan and guthka. Taking Mushtaque's hand, he led him out of the room. A strange sense of shame and humiliation washed over Mushtaque. His head felt heavy and his legs shook. Soon they were outside the hotel. Walking beside Quadir, he felt as if a soiled and smelly rag was clinging to his body. He wanted to get away, but Quadir appeared to be in no hurry to let him go.

"Come, let's go somewhere and slake our thirst," he said.

Mushtaque had tasted beer once quite some time ago at an office party. Now he had his first taste of whiskey in Quadir's company at Hotel Alibaba.

"What do you do in this company?" Quadir asked. He lit a cigarette and, holding it in the scissor of two fingers, brought it close to Mushtaque's lips. His eyes taut and glazed with three pegs of whiskey, Mushtaque stared into Quadir's eyes. Then, leaning forward, without touching it, he took the cigarette between his lips and pulled on it, Quadir style. The cigarette was damp from Quadir's lips. And Mushtaque smiled, saying nothing.

The next day, he went over and over all that had happened the night before. With disgust he remembered how he had dragged at Quadir's wet cigarette. Overcome with revulsion, he brushed his teeth and washed his mouth and lips repeatedly with soap.

But two days later, when the General Manager complimented him on his skillful handling of the situation, Mushtaque was overjoyed to hear the words of praise. The prospect of securing a permanent job at the end of his probation filled him with a sense of exhilaration. Problems like getting the ancestral house repaired and his younger sister married drifted before him like colourful balloons – along with feelings of disgust and repulsion.

The fingers which had once trembled while dialling Quadir's number now put the phone down on its cradle with the firmness of a new-found confidence. After that day it had been quite easy to entertain clients. He just had to call up Quadir. Quadir would procure the girl, Mushtaque would pay the money and the two of them would then go to a bar for a drink. Quadir always paid for the drinks.

Mushtaque came straight home from the office. As soon as he opened the door, he noticed the envelope lying on the floor. He recognized the writing at once. Picking up the letter, he went into his bedroom. Without taking his shoes off he sprawled on the bed and opened the letter. He had guessed right. It was from his father.

The doctors had diagnosed a cataract, his father had written. Amma was not satisfied with the local doctor's diagnosis, so he was coming to Bombay to get his eyes checked by some good eye specialist. At the end of the letter there were special instructions from Amma. Recite the Darud–sharif twice a day, before leaving for office and before going to bed. She had also urged him to feed a needy person once a month.

Mushtaque checked the date of Abbu's arrival. He was due the next morning! Mushtaque jumped up in panic. He kicked off his shoes, thrust his feet into slippers and went into the kitchen. Seven or eight empty beer bottles stood under the counter. A few whiskey bottles were lying in the bathroom. He gathered them all into a plastic bag, took it downstairs and handed the bag to the colony watchman who would, no doubt, sell them and buy himself half a bottle of country liquor. Suddenly Mushtaque laughed. His panicked reaction reminded him of his childhood. Whenever he had read a novel, hiding it between the pages of a textbook, especially during the exams, his ears would be pricked up, straining to catch Abbu's footfalls. The minute he heard Abbu coming he would hide the novel under his pillow or mattress ...

The train was late by two hours. Abbu was the last to appear at the compartment door. He was wearing spectacles with thick lenses and looked around with bleary eyes, seeking Mushtaque in the crowd on the platform. Mushtaque rushed towards Abbu and, after the salaam, took the suitcase from his hand. Abbu looked somewhat weaker than before, his beard was greyer and, from the small hesitant steps he took, Mushtaque realized that his eyes were badly affected.

In the taxi, as always, Abbu asked Mushtaque about his daily routine – when did he get up, when did he leave for work, when did he go to bed ... He sensed that Abbu was actually trying to find out whether the big city had made Mushtaque give up his namaaz.

When they reached the flat Abbu got a small metal plate out of his jacket pocket. "Your Ammi has sent this. It is the Yaaseen–

sharif, an important verse from the Holy Quran," Abbu said, handing it to Mushtaque. "She got it specially for you from the Majhanwanwale pir sahab. You must keep it in your pocket to be safe from evil. These words of the Almighty possess great power. If it is read at someone's deathbed then death comes without discomfort. Such is the grace of the Yaaseen-sharif that a patient may even be cured of his illness."

Mushtaque kissed the golden-edged plate devoutly and put it in his pocket.

Abbu took his clothes and towel and went to the bathroom. Lying in bed after his bath, Abbu surveyed the room. "Have you taken this flat on rent?"

"Yes. Two thousand, along with the phone." Mushtaque mentioned the rent without being asked.

"Two thousand for such a small place!"

He had known that Abbu would find the rent too high. He tried now to explain at great length the scarcity of houses in Bombay.

"Whatever you say, Mushtaque Mian, when I came to this city forty years ago, one could find a grand and spacious house for a thousand or twelve hundred! This is too much ..." Abbu mumbled.

"I'm still on probation. If the company approves of my work, I will be made permanent. They will give me a three-bedroom flat."

"May Allah grant you great success!" Abbu blessed him spontaneously. Then, remembering something, he said, "Negotiations for Guddi's marriage with Mateen Sahab's middle son are on."

"Ji!" Mushtaque replied in a feeble voice. He knew that Abbu would turn to his own marriage next. But Mushtaque was in no hurry to get married. He wanted to establish himself in his job first. That was much more important now. His apprehensions were justified. Abbu asked him what his plans were, then went on to point out the disadvantages of a late marriage and enumerate the advantages of a timely one. Mushtaque had heard this lecture often enough. In order to steer the conversation in a different direction he enquired about the mosque and madrasa in their mohalla. He had learnt to recite the Quran there from the hafiz sahab. Abbu was one of the trustees of the madrasa.

"Good thing you reminded me," Abbu said, getting up with great agility. From his suitcase he brought out a receipt book. Giving it to Mushtaque, he said, "Participating in the construction of a mosque or a madrasa is equivalent to building a palace in paradise. To enable you too to earn Allah's grace and blessings, by taking part in this noble task, I have brought along some receipts for donation towards the renovation of the mosque."

Mushtaque opened the receipt book. The receipts were made for twenty-five rupees.

"It's not much. Distribute them among the people you know. Twenty-five rupees is a small amount. It's quite easy to pay!"

Mushtaque could only nod in agreement. The few people he knew were his colleagues. Since most of them were non-Muslims there was no question of asking them for donations. But he said nothing to Abbu, whose face had lit up with the joyous thought of earning Allah's grace and favour.

Abbu had now been in the city for over a week. Mushtaque had taken him to an eye specialist who had told them that the cataract was not mature enough to be operated upon. They would have to wait for a few more months. Abbu wanted to return home the very next day, but Mushtaque had insisted that he stay a little while longer. Very soon he realized that it had been a mistake. He had to attend official parties and dinners. But he made it a point not to touch alcohol. When his colleagues insisted he said that he had a queasy stomach. He could never reveal to them that he didn't drink because of Abbu's presence. They might think he was an orthodox Muslim. At parties where people drank scotch he was ashamed of sipping a soft drink. In fact, when he had had beer for the first time, it was really to overcome this sense of shame.

That day too he was forced to drink to avoid an embarrassing situation. The annual office meeting was attended by an important senior government officer. After four martinis the General Manager whispered to him, "Call up Quadir. Our VIP guest wants complete entertainment."

The VIP guest, a high-ranking bureaucrat, was so intoxicated that he had to be helped by Mushtaque and Quadir to get to the hotel room. There, the uncouth middle-aged Bengali secretary reclined on the bed, puffing at his cigarette, while Mushtaque and Quadir waited for the girl to arrive. Mushtaque's ears caught the sounds of the departing cars. He tried to identify them ... this was the Managing Director's Toyota, that the General Manager's Maruti 1000 ... followed by the Project Manager's NE 118 ...

Half an hour later, a slim young woman entered the room. The Bengali secretary staggered to his feet and shook hands with Mushtaque. As he did so, Mushtaque felt a slight pressure on his shirt pocket ... The man had pulled out a packet of Dunhill cigarettes and was giving it to Mushtaque, at the same time motioning him out of the room. Mushtaque's hand curled into a tight fist of anger and loathing. Much as he wanted to, he couldn't even frown at the VIP guest.

On his way home in the taxi, he flung the pack of Dunhills on the road, as if he was slapping the commerce secretary hard. The taxi driver heard the packet fall to the ground and turned around to look at him. The driver's salt-and-pepper beard reminded him of Abbu. Despite promising him several times, he had not been able to take Abbu to visit his old acquaintances. Every night when he reached home and found Abbu sitting all by himself, he resolutely planned to take leave the next day and take Abbu out. But once he reached office he got entangled in phones and files and forgot his resolve. Abbu's desolate eyes behind the thick lenses pierced his heart – a heart which had become as hard as the wet tar road, completely unaffected by the ceaseless tread of heavy tyres on it.

Before turning the key to his door, Mushtaque checked his watch. It was a quarter past twelve. He tried to make his footsteps as light as possible while he changed his clothes and moved to his bed. But he was startled by Abbu's voice, "Mushtaque Mian!"

"Ji," he replied respectfully.

As was his habit, Abbu asked what time it was. And Mushtaque replied as he used to when he was a college student, telling him the time an hour before the actual. He heard Abbu softly reciting the Darud-sharif as he turned to the other side. Mushtaque lay down, facing the wall. Although his back was towards Abbu he felt ants crawling up his spine, as if Abbu had caught him reading the novel hidden between the covers of the textbook.

Mushtaque was in deep sleep when he felt his body being shaken and he managed to open his eyes. In the hazy light filtering through the window, he saw Abbu's silhouette bending over him, shaking him by the shoulder. Mushtaque got up immediately. His head was heavy and his mouth bitter. He rushed to the bathroom. He couldn't face Abbu in this condition. When he came out, a steaming cup of tea awaited him on the table next to the window. Abbu was sitting in the armchair, reading the morning Urdu paper. Abbu must have gone to the mosque for the fajr prayers and picked up the paper and milk on the way back, then made the tea, Mushtaque thought. He sat down and lifted the cup to his lips. With a start he realized that the tea had no milk. Instead, a slice of lemon lay on the saucer. He sensed Abbu's disapproving sidelong glances and began to perspire. He didn't regret missing the fajr prayer so much, but the cup of black lemon tea placed before him had overwhelmed him with a feeling of shame.

"I'm leaving today by the nine-thirty train."

Abbu's voice jolted him out of his thoughts.

"Today?" He looked at his watch. It was almost eight o'clock.

"Yes Beta, your Ammijaan must be getting worried. Besides Guddi's marriage negotiations have to be followed up."

"All right, Abbu. I'll just go and arrange for the ticket."

"I've already bought the ticket."

"You've ...!"

"Yes. I was doing nothing, sitting all by myself in this room, so yesterday I got it."

"If only you had told me, Abbajaan!" Mushtaque's voice was steeped in guilt and remorse.

"I can see how busy you are in your work, Beta. You come home so late, you don't even get enough sleep and have to miss your fajr prayers. I really do understand how busy you are."

Abbu's sentences stung him like arrows and the cup of black tea trembled in his hand. Abbu's remarks on his busy schedule and the fajr prayer made him furious with himself. I couldn't even spare some time for my father, he thought with despair. Abbu had to undergo so much trouble ... He cannot even see properly, yet he went all the way to the station ... Who knows how long he had to stand in the queue ...

Seeing Mushtaque absorbed in his thoughts, Abbu hesitantly said, "Those receipts for the school ..."

"Receipts ... Oh yes, of course! I've given out every single one of them. I even have the money ..." Not for a moment did he regret lying so blatantly to Abbu. In fact he was happy that he could fulfill at least one of Abbu's wishes. He took seven hundred and fifty rupees out of his pocket and gave the money to Abbu.

"My jacket is in the bedroom. Put it in the inside pocket."

Was Abbu pleased or was his smile sarcastic?

He found it difficult to decide. Quickly he stuffed the rupees into the pocket and came out.

Because of the traffic they reached the station barely ten or fifteen minutes before the train left. He found Abbu's seat in the compartment and pushed the suitcase under the seat so that Abbu could feel it against his legs. He got off the train, bought Abbu a bottle of mineral water and passed it to him through the window. When the whistle blew, Abbu touched Mushtaque's hand and advised him, "Beta, don't miss your prayers and remember that plate your mother sent. Keep it in your pocket always. It will help you stay away from evil."

Mushtaque could only nod his head. His eyes were filled with tears, but Abbu couldn't see the wetness. The train started moving and soon Mushtaque was left alone in the midst of the crowd on the platform.

Mushtaque came out of the station and looked around. Life went on everywhere, but it was soundless, involuntary, as if vehicles and people were being pulled by ropes, this way or that.

When he reached home his legs were trembling and a whirlwind was blowing through his chest because he had tried to wash down the guilt and the remorse of being a useless son with three bottles of cold beer.

He somehow managed to take his shirt off and emptied the contents of his pocket on the table. His eyes fell on the brass plate beneath a crisp five hundred rupee note. For some strange reason he was overcome with a desire to weep. He put his hand out and moved it slowly forward, touching the plate as if it were a piece of burning coal. Then he grabbed it and slumped in his chair like a weary traveller. He didn't know why the tears kept flowing from his eyes. In the distance a train whistled continuously.

He didn't know how long he cried. When his eyes had, drop after drop, lightened the burden of his heart, he opened his fist and raised it to his lips to kiss the Yaaseen-sharif. He noticed the five hundred rupee note which had come out of his pocket along with the brass plate. Immediately he remembered the pressure he had felt when the Bengali secretary had shaken hands with him ... This is what it was! Filled with repulsion he picked it up gingerly and dropped it at one end of the table.

He leaned back against the chair and closed his eyes. A deep sense of peace jumped into the four-walled boundary made of red bricks, and began to pluck raw mangoes for Guddi from the tree that stood in the mosque's compound. His small bare feet pattered in the courtyard of his house as he aimed his catapult at squirrels that scurried up and down the guava tree. Don't do that Beta Mushtaque, don't hurt the innocent ... Ammi was scolding him ... Tring, tring ... tring, tring ... Ammi's sweet voice mingled with the ringing of the phone ...

He opened his eyes, cast a disgusted look at the phone ... It must be the General Manager, he thought. Tring, trring ... trring ... The phone kept ringing. The General Manager always wanted a report when an important client had been entertained. Trring ... trring ... the vibrations of the bell crept up his skin, into his pores ... Trring, trring ... echoed in the hollow of his stomach ... rrring ... His hand reached out and put the receiver to his ears.

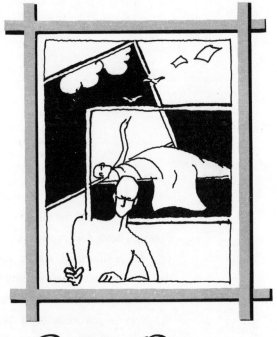

Self-Obituary

Joginder Paul
translated by Atanu Bhattacharya & Dipli Saikia

*N*o matter how often you presume that you have died, you cannot die until you are really dead. As for me, during the time I have been writing stories – almost half a century now – I have lived the lives of my characters rather than my own. So it seems that all that has happened to me, wherever and whenever, has happened only during the death of my "self" and therefore I have no embarrassment at writing a self-obituary. Another point: as a writer, I am not unaware that even the dead have to live to complete their stories. Which is why I don't find it unnatural to live beyond the realm of this life. Unable to find me in my own self, some of my acquaintances complain: "We do not know where you exist!" Where indeed? In the body of any one of my characters! If you want to meet me, start looking for that character in your mind. Or simply pray to Bhagwan to bless my soul, saying – if you choose – What a wonderful man he was!

From the very beginning life unfolded itself to me like a story.

During my childhood, I used to rise in my dreams and start walking to who knows where. My poor, illiterate parents decked their rajkumar with a two and a half masha gold ring because Pandit Dinanath had told them that gold was a lucky metal and that wherever the wearer might go, he would be safe. Bhayaji even wanted me to wear murkis in my ears but, when he finally saved some money for it, his asthma confined him to bed and the money was spent on his treatment. Anyway, among other things that transpired due to our poverty, I could no longer afford sleepwalking. I became an insomniac and thus, in this dreamless state, my parents grew old, and I – after indifferent studying – grew up.

And then?

And then the country was partitioned and the soil in which we were moored disappeared from under our feet. It was during this commotion -- I remember distinctly – that I was murdered and I drifted on to the shores of a New India from those of the Old, cloaked in some unknown identity. And though both my bearing and my mind were those of a slave's, Pandit Nehru's speeches in the newspaper convinced me that I was an independent citizen. Despite the fact that we did not own even a hole for shelter in the

This essay was first published as "Khud-Wafalia" in Urdu in the quarterly *Aqdar* (1993). It has been translated from a Devanagari transcription of the original text.

new country, we shouted slogans to declare we were masters of the whole land.

At long last, we found a dilapidated house in a tumble-down gali in Ambala. In one of the rooms was the grave of a renowned fakir. This green-clad, white-bearded darvesh was famous for rising from his grave after midnight and wandering around all the rooms before the crowing of the cock to see whether the dead were sleeping peacefully.

We had barely settled in this house when a merchant from across the seas made an unexpected appearance with his daughter, and struck a straight deal to carry my doli to British East Africa, where I would be employed in a government school with a hefty pay packet in spite of my third division in BA. After selling skimmed milk in Ambala for a while, I had started feeling that I was destined to do so in all my subsequent lives too. Thus, though finally liberated from British domination, I gleefully looked forward to becoming a rueful part of an insignificant rung of the British bureaucracy. I consider it my meanness – an honest, ethical meanness – that I took a photograph of mine in which I was seated in my baby Fiat outside my beautiful flat, filled with pride, and posted it to my old friends in India. Arre! They would be surprised and would whine for having been unable to break their fetters of freedom.

But, during this period, the Africans in Kenya were restless to break their bonds of slavery. The English are very particular about their rules and regulations. So they had drafted rules that established their dominion firmly. The Asian business ethic was such that a shopkeeper did not mind as long as you paid him handsomely, if you threw in a couple of ugly abuses as well. The plump Asians and the tough Europeans zealously guarded what they regarded as their ancestral legacy. But the black people were fed up of hunger and disease. They had no scruples in breaking the rules. If and when an opportunity to kill someone presented itself, they did not bat an eyelid for the victim would have enough money on him to sustain them for the day.

It was during my stay in Kenya that I wrote and, I should say, also failed to use fully the possibilities of an excellent story entitled "Jambo, Rafiqi" (Hello, My Friend). In it, one African is heading towards the shore from the interior of the country and another is moving to the interior from the coast. Both alight from their trains at a Voi junction to refresh themselves, and meet near a tap.

> "Jambo, Rafiqi"
> "Jambo"
> "Where are you going?"
> "Outside."
> "Where are you coming from ?"
> "Inside."
> "Why are you going in outside?"
> "In search of a job."
> As he sprinkles some water on his face, he feels
> hungry. "Do you have anything to eat?"
> "Yes. Have this."
> He takes out a slice of bread from his pocket.
> "It was a full loaf. I stole it from a Mahindi's stall at
> the last station."
> Both of them laugh.
> "And where are you going, Rafiqi?"

Mahindi: Indian.

"Inside."

"Where are you coming from?"

"Outside"

"Why are you going inside?"

"In search of a job."

In a country where jobs were reserved for foreigners even before they arrived, the locals were left to become thieves or dacoits or domestic help. The domestic help were often sent to jails from their servant quarters because they used to shelter thieves. To tell you the truth, although a person from very humble origins, I had never been aware of the pangs of poverty and helplessness to this extent in India. At the time of his death, a man just dies. You cannot expect a dying person to brood over the philosophy of death.

However, for fourteen years, on the substantial salary of a school master, I spoke out loud in impeccable English about character and morality to my students. Finally, at the age of thirty-eight or thirty-nine, voluntarily came back to India, fortified with my pension. Till I got a job here, I found two things especially amusing about my situation. Firstly, at such an advanced age, I was unemployed; and secondly, at this young age, I was already a superannuated person.

In the meantime, a Delhi weekly had advertised for the post of senior sub-editor. I went for the interview dressed in one of my best suits from Kenya. The chowkidar at the door stood up respectfully when he saw my smart attire, but when I told him about the purpose of my visit, he smiled as if to suggest, Oh! I thought you had come to employ somebody.

The khadi-clad owner of the newspaper had been a Raibahadur

during the British Raj and was currently a senior member of the ruling party. He informed me that he was looking for just the right person and had conducted long and comprehensive interviews, inviting only one candidate in the morning and one in the evening.

Finding him so immersed in his own words, I sat down on a chair without asking his leave. Suddenly, he asked me why I had left such a good job in Kenya and come here. I opened my mouth to answer him in colonial English but stopped, sensing a certain hypocrisy in my voice.

"Yes, please. Go on," he said, but continued to speak himself. "Perhaps you want to serve your country?"

I started laughing to myself. No. I actually laughed!

"Why are you laughing?"

How could I tell the Raibahadur that I had just been in my classroom, asking the students to write an essay entitled "If I were the Prime Minister of India."

The Raibahadur was annoyed. "Look! If you are appointed here, your stories will be of no use to me. I am chairman of several organizations. Listen carefully: first you will have to write down speeches according to my wishes and without my help. Second, you will be a kind of cultural secretary to me and all my responsibilities in this field will be entrusted to you. Third, though I am the Chief Editor of this weekly, it is you who will perform all the work. I shall only decide on policies.

"Fourth," I said to myself, "I do not want to work here."

"Then why have you come?" The Raibahadur's manner indicated that he wanted to say, To show-off your expensive suit? You had better go back to your Kenya.

Facing one disappointment after another, I seriously started thinking of going back to Kenya. But the British were no longer ruling Kenya that I might again plead with my resourceful brothers-in-law to get me a job there.

Not for nothing have historians labelled Muhammad Tughlaq mad for shifting the props of his kingdom from Delhi to Aurangabad. Lunatics are people like me, who commence their journey without a destination in mind. Wherever they arrived, they would convince themselves that that was the place they had wanted to come to. After reaching Aurangabad from Delhi, in fact, I immediately persuaded myself that this was the unfamiliar destination for which I had left Nairobi. The place looked so familiarly unfamiliar, as if I had carved it out of my imagination and then possessed it. They say, No one knows where we go after death. Where else? We always go back to the spots where our cherished links with life were. I feel that, wherever I am, I am buried under the soil of Aurangabad. This city has so many graves that I am certain it will be the liveliest place on the day of Qayamat.

The city of Aurangabad has been dug up so often in the last few decades, that one feels human beings have lost something immensely valuable here and, in their search for it, will reach the netherworld. The locals cautioned me, soon after I arrived, to tread gently, for beneath their feet their past flourished.

Their ancestors had been ceaselessly excavating, peeping, prodding, listening till they discovered centuries of their buried past. The first time I entered the Ellora caves, I felt as if I was but a shadowy thought of our ancient gods and goddesses. They spared me a wink and, finding me too insignificant for attention, immersed themselves in their own routine.

In this truly ancient city, under every house another lies buried.

When my house was being constructed, a friend told me, If you don't believe it, dig and see for yourself. When the ground near my front door was dug up a little, I actually saw, through an opening, a large reservoir lying underneath. Looking at the elders in this city, one always had the feeling that the old traditions settled below have come to the surface. These elders – like the late Maulvi Yakub Usmani and Govind Bhai Shroff – were embodiments of old-world virtues, of human goodness. The late Maulvi was never tired of doing good work in the name of Allah, and Govind Bhai in the name of Bhagwan. My close association with these two noble souls made me understand how a truly secular person could be saintly and how a true saint perfectly secular.

I believe there is some logic behind all the events of our lives – good and bad – but it is only coincidentally that some of them seem more significant than others. Take for instance, Shroff Bhai's selecting me for the post of Head and Professor of the English Department during those turbulent days just because I was unable to get even the post of Junior Lecturer! When the Head of the Department of English at Osmania University was explaining to me why he could not send me the interview letter because of my third class at BA, Shroff Bhai – with his Gandhi cap on and dwarfed in his loose dhoti-kurta – was keenly listening to us. And before I could return home, he was trying to convince my wife that we should all accompany him to Aurangabad. My wife was telling him that we did not want to leave Hyderabad since we were tired of roaming from place to place.

When we settled down in Aurangabad, my mother, who had been ill since our Nairobi days, lost her mental equilibrium. She had had a successful femur bone operation but the pain in the femur bone had travelled to the brain and she was not herself any more. In the magical silence of midnight, the doors of the ruins would start rattling and the shrieks of some spirit would be heard. From a distance at first, then from close by and then right here ... Who is it? Who? Ma! Be quiet. Calm down Ma! Ma! Quiet! Go to sleep ... And Ma finally closed her eyes. And we, my wife and I, thanked Bhagwan that Ma had finally found peace. We had found peace too and we started crying, overwhelmed by our relief, and our children and neighbours cried too. When we came back after the funeral rites, she emerged from our hearts and cooked many different types of delicacies for us. We ate our fill and did not wake up even after the sun was overhead. The dead do not have to wake up – Ma! Ma! I have died too. Can't the dead see the dead? Ma, where are you?

My friends often ask me, "Do you know how many stories of yours have been completed by your mother?" What can I say to them? Ma always used to say, "You sit down. You are good for nothing. I'll do whatever has to be done." Really, Ma did everything for us. Most of all for Bhayaji who was simple and poor. Had he not been so innocent, he would have been a writer like me. When he passed away, Ma turned all her attention to me, then to my children who have probably forgotten the person who nurtured them. And, in the process, she went mad and never looked like her old self to us. And before we could get to make up our minds, she had, in her state of madness, made up hers and left us, never to return.

I ask myself frequently: Why have I spent my life with such a sense of guilt? Was it because life repeatedly told me that if I wanted to get ahead, I should step back honourably? Was it because

I had not zealously followed the values which I had learnt from my experiences? ... Even if you are dying of hunger, you should look contented – which is why I am afraid of being caught whenever I extend my hand towards my favourite food ... If you have to thrash someone, thrash your desires – thrashed time and time again, my desires have been suffering from chronic swelling ... Always ask forgiveness for your crimes – when have I seized an opportunity to commit a crime? ... A decent man always keeps his hands folded – the chains around my hands broke long ago, but my hands remain folded ... Instructions! Advice! Experience is one thing, advice quite another. So what else could have happened other than what did? I kept running from life, and lived clandestinely, absently. And this is a death, isn't it? But how could I have written stories without dying?

Stories? Many of my learned friends burst into peals of laughter at the mention of stories. "Come bhai, we'll make him happy. Let him tell his stories first." These stupid intellectuals fail to comprehend that even the best lessons mean nothing unless they are presented through an incident. They are meaningless without a context. Had it not been for this, the same truth would not have acquired new meanings when born anew out of a new contextual reality.

During my stay in Aurangabad, the Nai Kahani was much discussed. It was quite natural for all young writers to set out in search of new possibilities in fiction. But in our enthusiasm of freely walking in step with Fiction in its own natural environs and, thus, experiencing it, we followed it in the armoured car of scholarship to hijack the poor thing to our universities where we wrote books from books, rather than life. However, the one happy aspect which resulted from this sad exercise was that the well-read and the learned were now also seen among writers. All this while, virgin stories fought shy and would not venture to step outdoors for fear of contact. And, when the time of contact became possible, the younger generation of writers had already lived half their lives. Never mind! The pleasures of union are perhaps more enjoyable when granted as a gift of maturity.

At last, when writers of my generation unburdened their heads, now going grey, of their heavy turbans and turned to life bareheaded, they were so excitedly ruffled at the sight of the familiar and the unfamiliar. They experienced events, the truth of which they did perceive but did not know how to arrest creatively. There were no standard models to guide them on their way. It was, therefore, not surprising if they lost their way, unpaved as it was. Yet, had it not been for their devotion and apostasy, how could they have found themselves driven to new shores? Columbus could hope to discover the new world he did only because of the stray waterways hitherto unknown to him. I regard my creative involvement, while in Aurangabad, very significant for this reason.

Lost in a storm, I know it for certain that I could not have escaped seeing new islands of flickering lights, where, on safe landing, I experienced such of my stories as "Kachhua," "Bazyaft," "Rasai," "Bazeech-e-Atfal," "Peechhe," "Rabt ka Inaaqad," "Jadoo," "Back Lane," "Panahgah" and "Teesri Duniya" ... In fact, quite a few other stories are pushing forward to complain, "I too." My problem then was that, like them, I too continued to stress the "I" in me.

We don't even think of Maharishi Valmiki when we read the

Ramayana. Our minds focus on Ramji. Who knows who had composed the slokas of the Gita in the Mahabharata? The moment one hears them one is lost in the all-pervading music of Krishna. But perhaps I could realize my smallness only because I was small. If I were someone big, how could I have realized the smallness in me? My critics may have had a different logic in not losing any opportunity to puncture my inflated state. But even though it was punctured and threadbare, I kept running at a gallop.

But for this experience, I would have lost the chance to free myself from my "I"-ness: I would not have realized how our creator presents us with only his creation. Why is he completely absent from the universe? As it were, creative writing also comes into existence when the creative writer is unaware of himself and chants of you and you alone ... I thank Bhagwan for the awareness of my own death, which put me on varied paths of life.

If I had not left Aurangabad after all those years there, my wife believed – and I agree with her – that my employers at the college would have been extremely disappointed in spite of their acknowledgement of my work and their love for me. Some of them believed, though they never said it, that my being a non-Marathi would hamper their future plans. If you come to think of it, providing leadership to this University – which in the eyes of the locals was a symbol of Marathi language and culture – I should have included the learning of Marathi in my list of responsibilities. But it is also true that I successfully managed to get my work done through English, Urdu and affection. My inability to speak Marathi never affected my relationship with my students and staff. The language of love reaches all hearts. On the other hand, people speaking the same language often cannot communicate with one another because of a lack of understanding amongst themselves. As an artist, I have always had an aversion to the interference of words. In both art and life, discourses take shape only when words are cloaked and everything takes place at the level of action and experience.

As a matter of fact, it had become important for me to leave my job because my unwritten stories kept haunting me like ghosts. My students never accepted my leaving the college. One of them said what was being observed by the renowned Structuralists of Europe for sometime, "Stories too write themselves, Sir."

Believe me, I remember all my four previous births exactly. First I was born in Sialkot and lived till I was 22. Then I was born in the city of Ambala and, when I was about one and a half years old, I died and opened my eyes in Nairobi. During my fourth birth in Aurangabad, one of my friends, Professor Saifuddin Siddiqui, told me that my ancestors must have lived in Aurangabad at some point of time and were buried there. Otherwise why should I have crossed the seas to settle down in that remote place? The murals of Ajanta and Ellora depict a whole horde of ordinary people. I gaze at each face and wonder if he was not one of my earliest forefathers who, disregarding all values, came here merely to satiate the hunger in his stomach and joined the armies of Krishna or Kansa. And now, in my fifth life, I have taken birth here in Delhi. I must have been here in one of my previous lives, for everything looked familiar, as if the same things presented themselves to me in an altered form.

Delhi throws out those who have no money. I could not have

stayed here either. But, within a year of my arrival here, I got a letter from London informing me that from the age of fifty-five, the pension of my fourteen-year job at Kenya would be increased so substantially that I would get much more than my salary as Principal in Aurangabad. And yet we don't believe that the rewards of our previous birth are enjoyed by us in this one. And in my case it also happened that what I had seen in the previous life, I wrote about in the context of my present one.

Machokos is situated just a few miles from Nairobi. In a blind house there, the blind eyes on pitch dark faces were imprinted in my mind and, many years later, in the dreadful darkness of contemporary India, the entire country appeared to me like that blind house. We, in spite of our eyes, were blind by habit. That is how I started my novel *Nadeed* – groping, feeling my way about in the dark, writing about what I had experienced. After reading it, a friend of mine told me that at first one cannot find a way to enter the novel and then, when one does find a clue to the entry, there is no coming out of it. He would definitely not advise any reader to take it up.

The one luxury I now enjoyed in Delhi was the time I got for my stories. That is why all of my time was spent outside the home and news of my well-being was conveyed to my friends only through my characters. Whenever my critics meet me, they immediately ask why my characters are so oblique, even impossible. What can I say? Critics refer to the word "Reality" in a very specific sense of the word. The truth is that every event or character in a story is neither credible nor incredible by itself. Their credibility can be adjudged only in the context of the story, just as that which we encounter or experience is only relevant to our own life. If a character in a story really starts to breathe and live in the story then, in spite of appearing absurd on the surface, he is actually real and makes the story move.

About five years ago, while offering my collection *Khula*, I was undergoing the creative tension of wanting my stories to flow out of the book and merge with the world indistinguishably. The stories in this collection – "Ifreet," "Bu," "Dadiyaan," "Koi Najaat," or "Bashinde" – and the later ones like "Khodu Baba ka Maqbara," "Muhajir" or "Shayad," introduced me to fictional potentials entirely new to me. In any case, I have to continue to come to grips with the future intrigues of life, even after my death. Whatever life I have had was that of my characters. Now, having died, I would take shelter in the existence of future writers for fulfilment.

The whole point is that I do not know when I died. I still breathe. Perhaps it is not me, but I am that character who lives eternally, changing name and appearance, and who laughingly explains to people: It is a simple matter, don't let Death ever overtake you.

About Joginder Paul

Born on September 5, 1925 in Sialkot, Joginder Paul migrated to India at the time of the Partition. After some years of living in Ambala, he went to Kenya where he served in the Ministry of Education for fourteen years. After his return to India in 1964, he joined S B College in Aurangabad (Maharashtra) as Head of the Department of English. A year later, he was appointed Principal of the same college. He resigned in 1978 and moved with his family to Delhi, where he could devote more time to his writing.

Joginder Paul has to his credit two novels, three novellas and many short stories and "short short" stories – a genre enriched markedly by his contribution. Acknowledged as one of the leading Urdu writers of the subcontinent, his fiction has received much critical attention. His writings have been translated into various languages including Norwegian, Russian, English, Hindi and almost all the other major Indian languages.

Among the many awards that Joginder Paul has been honoured with are the Urdu Adab Award (1983), the Modi Ghalib Award for Urdu Prose (1989), the Shiromani Urdu Sahityakar Award (1991) and the All-India Bahadur Shah Zafar Award (1996).

Joginder Paul's Works

Novels

1. *Ik Boond Lahu ki* (1962)
2. *Nadeed* (1983)

Novellas

1. *Amad-o-Raft* (1975)
2. *Bayanat* (1975)
3. *Khwabrau* (1990)

Collections of Short Fiction

1. *Dharti ka Kaal* (1961)
2. *Rasai* (1969)
3. *Mitti ka Idrak* (1970)
4. *Laikin* (1977)
5. *Bai Muhavara* (1978)
6. *Bai Irada* (1981)
7. *Joginder Paul ke Muntekhab Afsaane* (1987)
8. *Khula* (1989)
9. *Khodu Baba ka Makbara* (1994)
10. *Joginder Paul ke Afsaanon ka Intekhab*

Collections of short short stories

1. *Silvaten* (1975)
2. *Katha Nagar* (1986)

Non-fiction

1. *Rabta* (1997)

The Contributors

Abdul Naseeb Khan is a research scholar in the Department of English, Jamia Millia Islamia, New Delhi. He translates from Urdu to English and vice versa, reviews literary books and writes poems in English and Urdu.

Ameena K Ansari, a senior lecturer in the Department of English at Jamia Millia Islamia in New Delhi, graduated from Sophia College (Ajmer) and did her MA from AMU and her MPhil from Kashmir University. She has published a number of articles and book reviews in various literary journals and is currently preparing a course book on the English Novel for IGNOU. Interested in the act of translation, she hopes to do more of it, as well as write short stories.

Ashfaque Ahmad is a Pakistan-based writer of short fiction in Urdu. He also produce serials for Pakistan Television.

Atanu Bhattacharya, a senior research student of English Literature at Jawaharlal Nehru University (New Delhi), occasionally translates fiction from Hindi into English. He has been involved in several workshops on translations conducted by Katha in colleges in Delhi.

Dipli Saikia is a postgraduate student of English Literature at Lady Shri Ram College, New Delhi. She has also worked as a sub-editor for *Asian Age* and as a copy-editor at Katha.

Naghma Zafir teaches English at Zakir Hussain College, Delhi. She has worked for the United States Information Services as a translator and translates fiction and critical writings from Urdu into

English. Some of her translations have appeared in *Urdu Canada*, *Urdu Alive* and *Kavi Bharati*.

Qamar Rais is, at present, in Tashkent as a Cultural Representative of the Government of India. A former professor of Urdu at Delhi University, he is a pioneer of Progressive writing in Urdu.

Sajid Rashid is a young writer based in Mumbai. A journalist of repute, he brings out the Urdu quarterly *Naya Waraq*.

Sukrita Paul Kumar is a reader in English at a University of Delhi. Formerly a Fellow at the Indian Institute of Advanced Study, Shimla, she has also received the Shastri Indo-Canadian Faculty Research Fellowship (1993-94). She writes poetry in English and has three collections to her credit – *Oscillations*, *Apurna*, and *Folds of Silence*. Apart from a number of papers in literary journals, her publications are *Man, Woman and Androgyny*, *Conversations on Modernism*, *The New Story* and *Breakthrough*. She held a solo exhibition of her paintings at the AIFACS gallery a few years ago and was awarded the Bharat Nirman Award in 1991 for her contribution to literature and art.

Sunil Trivedi, a senior executive in a large public sector undertaking, has a keen literary sensibility. He was educated in Calcutta and Allahabad and is involved in a serious study of Hindi, Urdu and English literature. His knowledge of different languages (including Sanskrit), combined with his sensitivity to literature, make him a very competent translator.

Wazir Agha, in addition to being the editor of a leading literary journal in Pakistan, is also a distinguished Urdu poet and critic. He has contributed immensely to creating a distinctly "modern" critical and creative climate in Urdu literature through his writings as well as his magazine *Auraq*. His poetical works include *The Evening and Shadows, The Yellow Mountain of the Day, Half a Century Later* and *Butterflies in the Grass*. Among his critical works are *Satire and Humour in Urdu Poetry* and *The Native Genius of Urdu Poetry*.

ABOUT THE EDITOR

Keerti Ramachandra has an MA in English Literature from Karnataka University and an MPhil in Linguistics from Jawaharlal Nehru University, New Delhi. She has varied teaching experiences from remedial English to spoken/conversational English, English as a foreign language for non-Indians, graduate classes in Literature and Communication skills and high school courses. A close associate of Katha, she has edited *Visions-Revisions* (volumes 1, 2) for the organization, as well as *YuvaKatha* (volumes 5-8). Fluent in Marathi, Kannada and Hindi, she translates from all three into English and is a recipient of the A K Ramanujan Award for Translation (1995).

About Katha

Katha is a registered nonprofit organization working in the area of creative communication for development. Katha's main objective is to spread the love of books and the joy of reading amongst children and adults, with activities spanning literacy and literature.

Kalpavriksham, Katha's Centre for Sustainable Learning, develops and publishes quality material for neo-literate children and adults, and works with teachers to help them make their teaching more creative. It also publishes learning packages for first-generation schoolgoers and adult neo-literates. Specially designed for use in nonformal education, every quarter, Katha brings out *Tamasha!*, a fun and activity magazine on development issues for children, in Hindi and English. The *Katha Vachak* series is an attempt to take fiction to neo-literates, especially women. *Stree Katha* and *Stree Shakti* are illustrated, information-packed, interactive books on women's issues in a number of Indian languages.

Katha-Khazana, a part of Kalpavriksham, was started in Govindpuri, in one of Delhi's largest slum clusters, in 1990. Kathashala and the Katha School of Entrepreneurship have over 1000 students – mostly working children. To enhance their futures, an income-generation programme for the women of this community – Shakti-Khazana – and the Khazana Women's Cooperative were also started there, again in 1990.

Katha Vilasam, the Story Research and Resource Centre, seeks to foster and applaud quality fiction from the regional languages and take it to a wider readership through translations. The Katha Awards, instituted in 1990, are given annually to the best short fiction published in various languages that year, and for translations of these stories. Through projects like the Translation Contests, it attempts to build a bank of sensitive translators. Katha Vilasam also functions as a literary agency and works with academia to associate students in translation-related activities. It is working, specially through KathaSouth, to develop syllabi and teaching material for courses in translations. Katha has also been conducting workshops for teaching and reading translations in schools and colleges all over the country as part of the Kanchi Project, launched this year. Soon to be released are books in the Approaches to Literature in Translation series, which aims to provide texts for courses in translation. KathaNet, an invaluable network of Friends of Katha, is the mainstay of all Katha Vilasam efforts. Katha Vilasam publications also include exciting books in the Yuvakatha and Balkatha series, for young adults and children respectively.